PATRICK CIRILLO & JOE GAYTON

The Brown Bomber

First published by Story Killer 2026

Copyright © 2026 by Patrick Cirillo & Joe Gayton

All rights reserved. No part of this publication may be reproduced, stored, or transmitted in any form or by any means, electronic, mechanical, photocopying, recording, scanning, or otherwise without written permission from the publisher. It is illegal to copy this book, post it to a website, or distribute it by any other means without permission.

This novel is entirely a work of fiction. The names, characters, and incidents portrayed in it are the work of the author's imagination. Any resemblance to actual persons, living or dead, events, or localities is entirely coincidental.

Patrick Cirillo & Joe Gayton asserts the moral right to be identified as the author of this work.

Patrick Cirillo & Joe Gayton has no responsibility for the persistence or accuracy of URLs for external or third-party Internet Websites referred to in this publication and does not guarantee that any content on such Websites is, or will remain, accurate or appropriate.

Designations used by companies to distinguish their products are often claimed as trademarks. All brand names and product names used in this book and on its cover are trade names, service marks, trademarks, and registered trademarks of their respective owners. The publishers and the book are not associated with any product or vendor mentioned in this book. None of the companies referenced within the book have endorsed the book.

First edition

ISBN: 979-8-9956883-1-0

Typesetting by Reedsy

This book was professionally typeset on Reedsy.
Find out more at reedsy.com

To Joe... Also to Steve, Slo, Bear, Dave, Mos,
and so many other legends in my life.

Contents

Foreword

My brother Joe and I first met Pat in the early eighties. We had all come west looking to have careers as writers in the movie business. I don't think any of us realized how much the odds were stacked against us, but we were young and naive — we didn't know what we didn't know — but with the optimism and can-do attitude that comes with youth, we set about forging our way through the uncharted, shark-infested waters of Hollywood.

Pat and Joe always had a determination and work ethic which I envied and admired. Setbacks didn't seem to bother them; their belief in themselves and their undeniable talent outweighed whatever obstacles were in their way. I watched from the sidelines as first Joe, and then Pat, not only sold their scripts but got them made into feature films.

Along the way Joe and Pat occasionally teamed up on projects. I was in the room when Joe got a phone call from his agent telling him that a script that he and Pat had written together had sold for a massive amount of money. Sadly, it ended up not getting made but it was a milestone in their careers...which brings us to *The Brown Bomber.*

The Brown Bomber was another spec script that Joe and Pat teamed up on. I don't remember the details of the history of it, but I remember thinking that it was a very unique take on an American icon. I also remember thinking that this one didn't sound like a "sure thing" conceptually; that Hollywood probably wouldn't "get it". Joe and Pat didn't care. They never cared about trying to hew their good ideas to what was popular at the moment. It was something that spoke to both of them and they had to write it, commerciality be damned.

When Pat told me that he had decided to write *The Brown Bomber* as a novella all these years later, I was emotionally gratified. My brother passed away three years ago, and I thought this book would be a wonderful testament to not only Joe's memory but Pat and Joe's working relationship living on after Joe's death.

There are certain figures in American life who eventually stop belonging entirely to history and begin drifting into myth. Joe Louis is one of them.

Even people who know little about boxing know the silhouette: the calm expression, the impossibly heavy hands, the quiet dignity. *The Brown Bomber*. A man who knocked out Max Schmeling and, for one brief moment, seemed to knock fear itself out of the American bloodstream.

But myths are dangerous things. Over time they flatten people. Sand off contradiction. Reduce flesh and blood into symbols simple enough to fit on posters, headlines, and old newsreels.

What Joe and Pat have done with *The Brown Bomber* is something much rarer and much harder. They have restored the man inside the myth while still preserving the mythic scale of the man.

This is not a conventional sports novel. Nor is it strict historical fiction. It operates in the territory occupied by great American legend-making — the place where history, folklore, memory, exaggeration, pain, and truth all begin bleeding into one another. The Joe Louis in these pages feels at once human and larger than human, which is perhaps the closest one can come to understanding what he represented to millions of Americans who lived through his rise.

The novel understands something essential about Joe Louis: that he carried a burden far heavier than the heavyweight championship. He was asked to embody patriotism in a country that often denied his full humanity. He was expected to inspire Black America while simultaneously making white America feel comfortable. He became a symbol of democracy abroad while segregation thrived at home. Every smile, every public appearance, every victory contained a negotiation with America itself.

And yet the book never reduces him to politics alone.

At its core, *The Brown Bomber* is about endurance. About the emotional cost of greatness. About a decent man blessed — or cursed — with extraordinary power in a violent world. It is about the loneliness of becoming an icon before you've fully had the chance to become yourself.

What struck me most while reading was the melancholy running beneath the spectacle. The novel understands that triumph and sorrow often travel together. That legends are built not only from victories, but from sacrifice, silence, restraint, and survival.

Joe Louis did not merely fight opponents. He fought history. He fought expectation. He fought the terrible weight of symbolism itself.

And like all true American legends, he paid for it.

- Tony Gayton

The Brown Bomber

Chapter 1

Las Vegas, 1974.

The fairway at Caesars Palace ran green and manicured under a sky that had bleached to a pale blue, and the shadow of the great hotel fell long across the first tee. In that shadow, a black man stood planting a red wooden peg into the clipped grass with careful, ceremonial slowness.

He was sixty. He moved like someone older. His shoulders were still broad, and his musculature was still impressive, but his joints were spent. Walking, he hitched in the hip. Standing, he stiffened at the knees. His hands were the hands of an old man now, the knuckles of his big right gnarled and swollen, the skin dark, knotted, and shining, where it had been split open and stitched closed a hundred times and then a hundred more.

He addressed the ball, feet planted, shoulders square, head still. He drew back his driver.

What rose off the tee was majestic.

The ball left the clubface with a crack, like a rifle report. The three white men waiting behind him jerked their heads up in unison and tracked the ball, and tracked it, and went right on tracking it as it sailed over 150 yards past their balls, split the middle of the fairway, and rolled to a stop so far out that none of them could even see it.

"Jesus," one of the men said finally.

The old man did not smile. He stepped off the tee and handed the driver to the caddy behind him without looking.

The caddies followed them down the fairway. Three were white, about the age you'd expect caddies at a Las Vegas country club to be. Twenty or so. The fourth was black. He was also twenty-ish, and he had a faded baseball cap pulled low in the front that suggested he was hiding something under it. He did not seem to be thinking about the round. His eyes were on the old man.

"How the hell does that old man hit the ball so far?" one of the white caddies asked, shaking his head.

The black caddy, whose name was Tommy Bowdin, had been waiting all morning for someone to ask. He answered without looking over.

"Don't you know who that is?"

"No."

"That's the greatest fighter in the history of the world." Bowdin paused, because the name deserved its own air. "Joe Louis... the Brown Bomber."

* * *

Showered and combed and dressed again in the gray gabardine suit that had been tailored for him in 1952 and still fit him, Joe Louis stepped out of the men's locker room and into a chauffeured cart that whirred him up the path toward Caesars Palace.

Behind him, concealed against a hedge, Tommy Bowdin waited until the cart was halfway to the hotel. Then he began to jog.

The doormen at Caesars waved Joe through like he was family. They called him *Champ, and* they meant it. He was a fixture here, and they would no sooner have stopped him at the door than they would have stopped the sunrise. He nodded back to them and said, "Thank you," quietly. He walked into the lobby with the weighted grace of a man who had been walking into rooms for forty years and knew exactly where the eyes were. The younger guests might not have known him, but he was instantly recognizable to anyone who had been around for a while. And not just the fight fans. All of them knew Joe Louis. He could see them elbowing their friends as he passed, alerting them of his presence.

A few beats later, the doormen watched a young black man in a caddy's vest walk through the door.

Joe turned down the long residential corridor toward his suite without appearing to hurry.

Tommy Bowdin, following, trod as quietly as he could. He rounded the final corner a few paces behind, and just as he lifted his foot to take his next step...

The wall hit him in the back of the head.

It was not the wall that had moved. A hand the size of a shovel had taken him by the jacket and driven him into the plaster, and the force of it knocked his baseball cap off his skull. Out from under it, unbound at last, sprang his full Afro, high and dignified and very much ready for the revolution.

The hand held him fast. The face above the hand was not the face of the old man on the tee. He seemed younger than that. This was a man who had destroyed the Nazi superhuman, Max Schmeling, in the most important sporting event of the century.

"Who the hell are you?!"

Bowdin swallowed. His voice came out higher than he wanted.

"Your caddy from today."

Joe held him for another beat. His big hand was a warm, living stone against Bowdin's collarbone. Then, slowly, he released him.

"You don't follow a man all quiet like that. He'll think you got trouble in mind."

"Sorry."

Bowdin bent, picked up his cap, and pulled it down over the Afro.

"Why have you been following me?"

"I — I'm a journalism major at UNLV. I was wondering if I could get an interview."

Joe looked at him for a long moment. Not with malice now.

"Why?"

"Because you're Joe Louis."

The old man let out a breath that was half a laugh and half something else.

"Son, nobody cares about me no more."

He turned and started away down the corridor.

Bowdin found his voice.

"I do, Joe."

And that stopped him.

* * *

The suite was comfortable without being fancy. The casino kept him in rooms that said, We remember you without the excess that Joe Louis had no appreciation for. There were two armchairs facing a low coffee table, and on the table, next to an ashtray, was a stack of room-service menus and a bottle. It was an old bottle. Tall and green-shouldered, with a label printed with a sailing ship and some words Bowdin couldn't read. The glass was the color of seaweed. The seal had been broken a long time ago.

Joe sat across from him, and Bowdin, sitting down himself, pulled a Sony cassette recorder out of his canvas shoulder bag. He set it on the table, lining it up neatly between them.

"You mind if I record this?"

"Suit yourself."

Bowdin pressed the red button. The little reels began to turn. He took a breath.

"So you prob'ly want to know about the Bum of the Month Club," Joe said. "All that jazz."

This was a test. Bowdin knew it was a test. The Bum of the Month Club was what the sportswriters had called it when Joe had defended the heavyweight title once a month, year after year, against any comer. In the early 1940s, it was a run so long and so dominant that it had stopped being a sport and become a kind of routine.

Bowdin did not want to write that article. That article had been written.

"Actually," he said, "I was wondering why you never joined the struggle."

Joe went very still.

"What struggle?"

"Civil rights movement. Brothers in the Panthers called you a 'Tom.'"

The old man's face did not change, but his attitude changed entirely.

"Get out."

"But —"

"I said, Get out!"

He came up out of the chair, and in the rising of him, Bowdin remembered, with sudden awful clarity, what this man had been. Bowdin fumbled for his recorder, nearly dropping it, and stood up. His afro grazed the lampshade. He began to back toward the door.

"Little punk with your clown-ass hair, don't know nothing!" Joe said. His voice had thickened. "I fought my battles."

Bowdin was about to leave, but he didn't want to be pushed out of a door by anyone, including Joe Louis.

"I'm not talking about in the ring."

Joe met his eyes.

"Neither am I."

And it was Bowdin's turn to go still.

The moment stretched. A pulse, then two.

"What battles are you talking about?" Bowdin asked very carefully.

The old man looked past him, out the window, at the Vegas afternoon, at the sun on the parking lot, at forty years of silence. When he spoke again, it was in a different voice entirely. Lower. Older. Sincere.

"Battles that ain't in no history books," he said. "Battles that were fought and won and never been talked about since."

Bowdin sat back down.

"Then maybe it's time you did."

Bowdin sensed it was safe to turn the tape recorder back on.

Joe looked at him. He looked at the bottle on the table. He looked a long while at the bottle. Then he reached for it and uncorked it and poured himself a small glass of the pale liquid, and the smell that came out of the bottle was caraway and honey and salt and something else — something that was not a smell so much as a memory.

"Want a snort?" he said. "Real good stuff. Norwegian liqueur."

"No, thanks."

Joe shrugged and did not insist. He took a small, ritual sip, and then he sat back in the chair. His shoulders seemed to lower an inch. He looked at Bowdin over the glass.

"That thing on?"

Bowdin nodded.

Joe smiled.

"I'll tell you a story," he said, "that'll straighten that nappy bush of yours right out."

He took another sip. He set the glass down.

"I was born in Lafayette, Alabama, County of Chambers, 1914."

He leaned back. The afternoon sun crossed the room, found the green of the bottle, and threw a small, surprising jewel of light onto the wall.

"I was round about one-year-old..."

* * *

Lafayette, Alabama, 1915.

The shack stood on the edge of a white cotton field that went on forever, dotted with dark-skinned people who picked the cotton with calloused hands. At night, the field rested to the droning song of the cicadas. The shack itself was boards and tar paper. Inside, it was somehow darker than outside.

In the back bedroom, six children slept. Four girls shared a single mattress on the floor, arranged like the pressed petals of a flower. Two boys slept close to each other on another mattress along the opposite wall. The air was warm and inert enough to stick to you.

And in the corner, in a crib his father had made out of what wood could be spared, lay a seventh child.

He was not quite a year old. His name was Joseph Louis Barrow, though nobody called him that yet. His mother called him "my baby" and sometimes "Lord have mercy," and his father called him "boy" with a tenderness he did not use for any other living thing. He had dark eyes that caught whatever light was available and held onto it. He had just learned to walk.

On this particular night, those dark eyes were open.

Through a split in the warped floorboards, something was arriving.

The brown and white striped body of a copperhead slipped up out of the dark. It had come in from the cotton field where the heat still lingered in the earth, following a trail of warmth that led it toward the sleeping children. It reached the base of the girl's mattress. It climbed.

The baby watched.

There was nothing in the baby's mind that had words. There was heat and softness and breath and the smell of kerosene, and there was that long, skinny thing that the baby knew didn't belong there. The baby did not know the word snake. He did not know the word danger. He knew only that this was wrong and that it was climbing toward his sister's face.

The copperhead arced up and met the girl's cheek, inches from her forehead. Its tongue tasted her.

What happened next would be retold as a story in the Barrow

family for the rest of their days, and nobody who had been in that room would ever quite agree on what the words should be. The telling that came closest was that the baby simply got up and handled it.

One moment, the snake tasted the air above a sleeping child. The next, it was in the right fist of the boy who had just learned to walk. The little hand had closed at the base of its head in a grip no one-year-old should possess, and the baby had turned the snake to face him, curious and unafraid. The snake, enraged by being held, bared its fangs at him.

The baby's dark eyes went from curious to cold. It was the first time in his life that this particular feeling would climb up out of him, though it would not be the last. It was not hatred. It was a quiet, clean disappointment in what the world planned to do to the people he loved.

He slammed the snake's head against the dresser. Once. It was enough. It was loud enough to wake some of the children, and they watched baby Joe drop the body to the floor. He wobbled. He had, after all, only learned to walk that week. He climbed up and over the rail and settled himself down among his blankets. Within half a minute, he was asleep again, as if nothing at all had happened.

* * *

Six years later.

By age seven, Joe was known in a quiet circle of swamp towns along the Alabama border as the boy who wrestled gators.

The show, such as it was, took place on Saturday afternoons on a patch of ground his father, Munroe, had cleared beside a still brown crook of water where a large bull alligator had been penned in. The crowd was always the same: the poor black men of the county, come to spend a dime on the only thing they would see that week that was not work. Some of them brought friends from town to witness the event and were paid two cents for recruiting new guests.

Munroe Barrow had done many things in his forty years on earth, most of them badly, but the one thing God had given him was the vocal rhythm of a circus barker.

"For ten cents!" he cried, high and jubilant, striding in front of the fence with his thin arms spread like a preacher's. "One thin dime! You are about to see the most amazing feat of strength and courage you ever witnessed! My seven-year-old boy, Joe Louis Barrow, will wrassle a f'rocious ol' bull gator that's more than ten times his weight!"

The crowd laughed and jostled. Dimes clinked into Munroe's tin can.

Seven-year-old Joe stepped into the clearing wearing only a pair of cut-off shorts. He was skinny, fifty pounds soaking wet, but the nascent muscles across his shoulders and thighs were already visible to anyone looking for them. In his right hand, he carried a coil of rough hemp rope.

He was not scared. He was annoyed that his father had to be such a showman. He was looking forward to getting in there with that alligator.

Among the crowd that day, standing a little apart at the periphery and taking no particular notice of the dimes, was a white man. He was twenty-five or thereabouts. He was already prematurely bald. He wore a neat linen jacket against the heat, and he held a small notebook against his thigh. He was not smiling. He was watching the boy, and only the boy, and now and then his pencil moved.

Nobody in the crowd spoke to him. Nobody ever did.

"Your boy is gonna get ate by that gator," said a man at the front of the crowd, happily.

"Ten cents," said Munroe, "and my Joe will prove you wrong."

The dimes kept clinking.

When the can was full enough, Munroe nodded to his son. Joe hopped the pine rail in a single clean movement, landed in the dust inside the pen, and turned to face the alligator.

The alligator was twelve feet long, and it did not like Joe at all. It opened its great mouth in a display that had stopped every other creature in the swamp for years. It hissed. Joe circled. The alligator turned to keep facing him, and the yellow eye that followed him was the eye of something that intended to eat him the moment he got bored.

The alligator decided it was time. It charged.

Joe sidestepped the creature, and as it shot past him, he threw himself bodily onto its back. Gasps went up from the crowd. The alligator thrashed and tried to roll him off, and the boy, impossibly, hung on.

The crowd was cheering wildly now. Cheering and stamping and slapping their thighs. They had never seen anything like it.

The bald man in the linen jacket made a small, careful note and said nothing.

It was at this moment that Lillie Barrow arrived.

She came up the dusty road, leading her four daughters like a general leading a column into battle. And she was furious.

"See, Mama, I told you he was doin' it again."

Lillie did not look at her daughter. She had found her husband, and she was advancing on him with a purposeful stride that could be read at thirty paces.

"Munroe Barrow," she said. "I warned you about letting my little baby boy wrassle gators!"

Her open hand met the side of his face with a pop that carried over the swamp.

"But the boy's got a gift, Lillie!"

"I'll give you a gift you won't never forget!"

She whacked him again.

So absorbed were Munroe and Lillie in the argument that neither of them was looking at the water when the alligator, furious at the indignity of being ridden, gave one mighty convulsion and plunged, taking Joe with it, down into the murky brown.

The crowd rose. They gasped. Lillie did not hear them.

"Mama!"

It was her eldest daughter, Vunice. She was pointing at the water.

Lillie turned. The surface of the water was roiling with bubbles, and of her son, there was no sign at all.

Without a thought for her own life, Lillie Barrow charged into the water, despite the fact that she could not swim.

She did not get more than two steps.

Joe Louis Barrow, aged seven, burst up through the surface of the swamp with the alligator clutched beneath one arm, holding the creature's head up for all to see. Around its snout, tied off tight, was the coil of hemp rope he had carried down with him. The alligator posed no threat.

The crowd went out of its mind.

Lillie Barrow did not cheer. Lillie Barrow waded in and caught her son by the arm and hauled him, dripping, to the shore, and as she passed her husband, she said, quietly and without heat:

"Last time I'm gonna warn you."

Munroe, duly chastened, watched them go. When Joe looked back at him over his mother's shoulder, Munroe winked. Then, once Lillie had turned the bend in the dirt road, Munroe drew from the bib pocket of his overalls a pint bottle of corn mash and, with a connoisseur's appreciation for the trouble he had just avoided, took a long, slow belt.

The bald man in the linen jacket folded his notebook shut and slipped it into his breast pocket. He did not stay for the drinking. He walked, unhurried, back up the dirt road toward wherever he had come from, and by the time anyone looked for him, he was already gone.

* * *

Ten years after.

Joe was seventeen. He had come into his height and his width at the same time, which was rare, and he had come into them all at once, which was rarer still. He had the narrow waist of a welterweight but the shoulders of a lumberjack, and when he reached into a cotton boll, the crisp white fiber seemed almost to leap into his fingers.

He picked faster than anyone in the family. He picked faster than anyone in the county or the state. The sun pressed down and did not touch him. He seemed, to his sisters working the next row over, to stand inside his own weather.

He filled a basket, handed it to the nearest sister and took her half-empty basket without asking, and kept going.

He was thinking about nothing in particular. That was the

thing people who knew him best would have told you about Joe: when he was working, he was not anywhere else. It made him very good at the work, and it would later make him very good at other things.

It was into this quiet that Leon came running with no shoes on and his eyes all whites.

Leon was eleven. He was the younger brother of Joe's cousin Adrian.

"Joe! Joe! They got my brother, Adrian! Gonna string him up!"

Joe set the basket down very carefully on the ground because he was not a man who broke things if he could help it. He straightened.

"Lead the way."

"Joe Louis Barrow," his mother called from the next row over, in a voice he knew and had always minded, "you stay right here!"

Just a glance for her. Just one. It held an apology and a decision and an I-love-you compressed into the two seconds it took for him to turn and follow Leon out of the cotton. And Lillie, who had raised him, understood all three and could do nothing about any of them.

The oak tree stood by itself in a clearing half a mile up the road. It was the kind of tree that had been used for this before. The rope was already thrown over a lower branch, twelve feet off the ground, and at the end of the rope stood Adrian Barrow, eighteen years old, a loop around his neck and his hands tied behind his back, and he was trying very hard not to beg.

The mob consisted of twenty white men from town. One of them sold Munroe his corn mash. Joe knew their faces well enough, and now he was going to remember every one of them for the rest of his life.

Their leader, whom Joe knew as Liberty Sikes from the tannery, was a big man in a denim shirt with sweat stains the color of old tea. Behind his back, he was called Libby, a name he hated.

"This'll learn you a lesson," Liberty exclaimed with his nose pinned to Adrian's face, "on how you look at a white woman, boy!"

"She come up to me!" Adrian said. He was trying not to cry. "I swear to God!"

"Don't you dare swear to my God!"

Liberty's open hand cracked across Adrian's already bloodied face. Adrian's head snapped sideways and back. A thin, bright string of blood hung between his teeth.

Liberty stepped back and raised his voice to the men holding the rope.

"Hoist his black ass up, boys!"

And they began to pull.

Adrian's feet left the ground. His eyes bulged. He reached for the rope with his chin, trying to get it under the loop, trying to buy a breath of air. The loop did not give. He began to gasp. His feet kicked, seeking earth that was out of reach even as he stretched his toes.

The men watching had the look on their faces that a mob gets when its blood finally drops into its throat. It was a look Joe would remember because he would see it again one day in newsreels out of Nuremberg, on the faces of the men cheering Hitler.

He came over the rise into the clearing at a dead run.

Nobody heard him coming.

He leapt.

The oak branch — twelve feet up, and thick as a man's thigh, the branch on which many of this mob's forefathers had hanged many of Adrian's forefathers, was torn off the tree. Joe Louis Barrow broke it off with his right hand the way you might snap off a piece of celery. The weight of him and the weight of the branch and the weight of Adrian, still tied to the other end of it, came down together. They tumbled into the dust in a tangle of limbs, rope, and bark.

Joe ripped the rope from Adrian's hands as if it were string.

Adrian, gagging, pulled the rope from his neck with fingers that would not stop trembling.

Joe Louis stood up.

The branch lay at his feet. It weighed, perhaps, two hundred pounds.

The mob had not yet moved.

Joe picked up the branch with one hand and then rested it on his right shoulder, the way a power hitter rests a baseball bat. The mob was staring at him. Their expressions had changed. They were starting, slowly, to understand that they were no longer the most dangerous thing in the clearing.

They started forward anyway. A mob, once committed, goes where it means to go.

Joe swung.

The branch met Liberty Sikes on the chin. Liberty folded at the knees and dropped in a heap. Two men beside him went over in Joe's follow-through. Four men on the other side of the swing flinched, and then, ashamed of flinching, lunged.

Pistols came out.

Joe moved before the pistols did. He dropped the branch, pulled Adrian in behind him with one motion, reached down, and snatched up the unconscious Liberty by the collar, and in the next half-second, the big man was in front of him, held up as a shield. One of Joe's hands clamped Liberty's throat, and the other wrapped around his chest. Liberty's eyes snapped open. Joe's thumb was under his jaw. The veins in the man's throat bulged.

Joe leaned into the Liberty's ear.

"How's that feel, redneck?"

Then, to the rest of the mob, louder:

"Lower them guns or I'll snap his neck."

They hesitated.

Joe, without looking away from them, spoke into Liberty's ear again.

"Libby, you tell 'em!"

Liberty's mouth worked. Nothing came out. Joe loosened his grip slightly. Air found his throat, and so did the words.

"Drop the guns!"

They still hesitated.

Joe tightened his grip again. Liberty made a sound that was not a word.

Guns fell to the dust. One, two, five, nine. One of them went off when it hit. A plume of earth jumped up at a man's boot.

Joe did not move.

"Now move on outta here," he said, "or he's a dead man!"

"You're the dead man!" shouted one of them. He was a red-faced man who stood toward the back.

"Ain't none of y'all man enough to come after me," Joe said. "Now git!"

He tightened his grip for emphasis. Liberty's face, which had been red, went purple. His eyes began to roll.

Slowly, and with sour reluctance, the men began to back away.

Joe called after them, his voice calm now, almost conversational. "When you get into town, ring the church bell so's I know you're there. Then I'll let him go."

They kept walking. The red-faced man broke off from the group and turned toward a pickup truck parked beside the oak. It was a dirty black Ford, the only vehicle in sight.

Joe's voice went flat.

"Leave that truck here, boy!"

"Not a chance!" the man shouted back and put his hand on the door.

Joe lifted Liberty one-handed, clear off the ground. Just the hand around the throat. The man's legs kicked in the air the way Adrian's had kicked not three minutes earlier, and it was exactly this echo, the feet pedaling on nothing, the body hanging, that made Liberty find the breath, somehow, to manage one last ragged gurgle.

"Damn it, Earl, leave the goddamn truck!"

The red-faced man, Earl, stood very still. His hand remained on the door. He looked from his dangling friend to Joe, and then back at his friend, and then, slowly, he took his hand off the door.

He turned and joined the others.

Joe watched them go. He did not set Liberty down, though his grip on the man's neck softened a shade so that he could, at least, breathe. Between the sound of the crickets and the sound of his own heart, Joe could hear, very faintly, the first stirrings of a long, eventful life coming his way.

Adrian, still sitting in the dust, rubbing at the rope burn on his throat, spoke first.

"You know they ain't gonna let this slide, Joe."

Joe looked down at the boy he had just pulled out of a noose.

At his own right hand, then at Liberty, who was nearly in tears from the ordeal.

"I know," Joe said.

Chapter 2

The church bell rang.

Joe heard it from two miles out, the sound rolling across the fields in the thick afternoon heat. He kept driving. The truck he "borrowed" from Earl bucked and shuddered over the dirt road, and he kept his foot down on the accelerator and his eyes fixed ahead.

In the passenger seat, his mother sat with her hands folded in her lap. She had not cried. She had not looked back at the shack. She sat straight, the way she always sat, her jaw set, watching the road unspool before them.

Munroe and the rest of the family were piled in the truck bed behind them, Munroe sitting with his back against the cab, the girls and their brothers tucked in around him. He had produced a pint bottle of corn mash from somewhere on his person and was working on it with quiet dedication. The kids, however, seemed happy to be on the road. Vunice started singing *I'll Fly Away.*

"*Some bright morning when this life is over, I'll fly away.*"

In the cab, Joe gripped the wheel. His right hand, the one that had closed around Liberty's throat and held a grown man off the ground by his neck, lay easy on the wheel now, relaxed, the knuckles still faintly red.

"I'm sorry, Mama," he said.

Lillie Barrow turned to look at her son. She studied his profile for a moment.

"You got nothing to apologize for, son. You done the right thing."

Joe kept his eyes on the road. The cotton fields on either side ran flat to the horizon, white and enormous, belonging to men whose names were on deeds Joe's family would never see.

"If I done the right thing," he said, "how come we gotta run?"

Lillie was quiet for a moment.

"Cuz the world just ain't ready for a black man like you. But someday that'll change." She paused. "You're gonna help it change. I just know it."

From the truck bed, Munroe's voice floated over the cab.

"Damn straight. My boy's gonna be a national hero."

Joe almost smiled. He heard the bottle tip.

"Just drink your mash, Munroe," Lillie said.

Joe's jaw tightened. He thought about Liberty Sikes' face going purple. Thought about the sound of displaced air that the man's feet had made, kicking at nothing, the same way Adrian's feet had kicked. Thought about the guns dropping one by one into the dirt.

"I shoulda just killed 'em all," he said.

"Quit that ugly talk." Lillie's voice was flat. "Just lowers you to their level."

"But it ain't fair for us to have to leave our home."

Lillie looked out the windshield. Her expression did not change.

"Home?" She let the word sit for a moment. "That place weren't never our home. White cotton farmer owns that shit shack." She paused. "'Scuse my French."

Joe glanced at her. The corner of her mouth had moved, barely, against her will.

He felt it too. Despite everything, despite the bell still ringing behind them and Adrian with rope burns on his neck — despite all of it, Joe felt the laugh start low in his chest.

"Good riddance, I say," Lillie said.

Joe looked back at the road.

"But where we going?"

"North," she said. "And don't slow down til we hit that Mason-Dixon line."

Joe punched the accelerator. The truck lurched forward, found its speed, and the shack and the cotton field and Lafayette, Alabama fell away behind them in a long cloud of red dust. The girl's singing seemed to erupt into a higher volume. Then Lillie started singing. Then Munroe joined in. He had a surprisingly good voice.

Joe just drove, smiled, and listened.

I'll fly away, fly away, oh glory. I'll fly away in the morning. Hallelujah, by and by, I'll fly away.

* * *

Detroit, 1932.

Detroit roared.

Even from the street, you could feel the city's pulse: the deep mechanical thud of the auto plants, the clatter of streetcars on their rails, the thousand overlapping sounds of a place that ran day and night without apology. The air smelled of exhaust, machine oil, and desperation.

CHAPTER 2

Black Bottom spread out along Hastings Street and the blocks surrounding it, the neighborhood that Detroit had assigned to its black citizens, who had arrived by the thousands from the South following the jobs that the plants offered. The buildings were old and close together. Ice trucks worked the streets in the early morning heat, stopping and starting, the drivers calling up to the windows above.

Joe Louis Barrow was in his late teens and could carry two hundred-pound blocks of ice, one in each hand, using iron hooks, as if they weighed nothing.

He pulled the blocks from the truck now. The ice was cold against his palms; the hooks bit clean and he went through the tenement doors at a pace that made the other delivery men stop and watch. Up the stairs he went, not two at a time or four at a time but six, the ice blocks never wavering, the stairwell echoing with his footsteps.

He worked the ice into the box outside the apartment door, his hands moving fast and sure, chips flying, and then he was back down the stairs and out the door and crossing to the truck before the ice chips had settled on the landing.

He did not notice the white man watching him from across the street.

The man was in his 30s now, bald, his pale scalp catching the morning sun. He stood at the edge of the sidewalk with a small notepad open in one hand and a pencil in the other, and he watched Joe with focused, patient attention. He wrote something in the notebook. Watched Joe go back into the building. Wrote something else.

Then the truck pulled forward, and a produce cart came between them, and the bald man was gone.

Joe was on his way back to the truck, the empty hooks over

his shoulder, when a man stepped out in front of him.

This man was almost as big as Joe, which was saying something, and dressed in a suit that had not come off any rack. The suit was charcoal with a faint chalk stripe, and it fit the man's shoulders the way a good suit is supposed to fit. He was 40 years old, or thereabouts, with a broad, confident face and an unhurried manner. He was accustomed to people making room for him.

He stepped directly into Joe's path.

Joe stopped.

"You want something?" Joe asked.

"That depends," the man said.

Joe waited. He had the ice hooks in his right hand, loose, not threatening, just present.

"Depends on what?" Joe said.

"How smart you are, Joe Louis Barrow."

Joe looked at him steadily. "How you know my name?"

The man spread his hands slightly, an easy gesture. "Oh, I heard all about you, boy. How big and strong and fast you are."

"I gotta get back to work," Joe said.

"How much are you making toting that ice?"

Joe regarded him for a moment. The man had not moved out of his path. He showed no sign of intending to.

"Twenty-eight cents an hour," Joe said.

The man tilted his head back. "Hoo-eee, you a regular John D. Rockerfeller!"

"The other guys only make twenty," Joe said. There was no defensiveness in it. It was just a fact.

"So, you work twenty times faster than them," the man said, "and only make forty percent more money. That's not smart."

Joe looked at him. "Mister, you're in my way."

The man reached into his breast pocket and produced a folded bill. He held it out flat on his palm. It was a hundred dollars.

"What if I told you I could make you rich inside of two years?"

Joe looked at the bill. Then, at the man. "I know about guys like you, and I ain't interested."

The man smiled. It was a good smile, warm and practiced and slightly dangerous. "What is it you think I do?"

"You're a bootlegger," Joe said. "I don't want no part of it."

The man laughed heartily. It was a laugh that could be heard across the street. "Ha. I make my money in the fight game."

Joe shifted the hooks to his other hand. "What's that got to do with me?"

"I didn't believe the stories I been hearing 'bout you 'round Black Bottom," the man said, "till I seen what you just did with my own eyes. I think you might just have what it takes to be a champion."

"Look," Joe said. "I gotta work."

The man held the hundred-dollar bill out again, patient, unhurried. "Twenty-eight cents an hour, you say?"

Joc noddcd oncc.

"One hundred dollars," the man said. "You'd have to haul ice for 357 hours to make that much."

Joe tried the arithmetic in his head. The numbers didn't come easily, but the shape of what the man was saying came through clearly enough.

"My mama says easy money is dirty money," Joe said.

"All you gotta do is walk over to the gym with me, and it's yours."

Joe looked at the bill. Looked at the man. Then he stepped around him and went back to the truck.

He did not look back. He could feel the man watching him as

he pulled the next two blocks from the ice shelf, hooks biting in, cold spreading up through his palms. He went into the building and up the stairs and did not think about the hundred dollars or the man in the chalk-stripe suit.

At least he told himself he did not think about it.

* * *

Quitting time came in the long light of late afternoon.

Joe walked away from the ice truck, his shirt dark with sweat and his hands numb at the tips from the cold. He turned up Hastings Street without thinking about where he was going.

He stopped in front of the gym.

It occupied the ground floor of a narrow building, the kind of building that had seen several uses and wore each of them with equal indifference. The front window was large, plate glass, and through it Joe could see the interior laid out in the yellow light: a ring, heavy bags hanging from the ceiling, a speed bag mounted on a platform in the corner, open floor space where fighters moved.

He stood at the window and watched.

The sounds came through the glass, muffled but present: the pocka-pocka of the speed bag working in its rhythm, the deep thud of fists on the heavy bag, the whir of the jump rope, the slap of feet on canvas. Two young men sparred in the ring, their trainers calling to them from the corners. Sweat flew from their hair as they worked.

Joe watched the fighters and felt something happen in his chest. It was not a thing he could have named.

He pushed through the door and went in.

The smell hit him first. Old leather, sweat, the sharp tang of liniment. The sounds that had been muffled through the glass were full and immediate now. The pocka-pocka of the speed bag was right there, the rhythm of it precise and hypnotic. Joe stopped just inside the door and stood with his hands at his sides.

The man from outside was John Roxborough. He was already moving toward him from across the floor.

"Joe!" Roxborough crossed the space between them with his hand out, smiling broadly, his voice carrying over the noise of the gym without effort. "Welcome, man! Got a fella I want you to meet."

"Offer still good?" Joe asked. "A hundred dollars."

He reached into his pocket and gave Joe the bill, and led Joe across the floor, past fighters who glanced up and then went back to their work. He stopped beside a man who was watching the sparring ring with the alert, tired eyes of someone who had spent decades watching men hit each other for a living.

Chappie Blackburn was fifty, small and wiry, his face a map of every dirty gym he had ever worked in and every boxing ring he had ever climbed out of. His hands, wrapped around the top rope, were scarred across the knuckles. He turned from the ring when Roxborough spoke.

"Chappie, I want you to meet Joe Louis Barrow."

The old trainer looked at Joe. "Joe Louis," he said, as if correcting the record.

They shook hands. Chappie's grip was dry and careful, a man taking inventory.

"Chappie is the best trainer in the business, Joe," Roxborough said.

Chappie's eyes did not leave Joe. "So," he said. "You're a fighter?"

"I haul ice," Joe said.

Chappie threw Roxborough a flat look. Roxborough ignored it.

"Chappie, I got me a hunch about this one here." He turned to Joe. "Joe, you ever hit a heavy bag before?"

"Nope," Joe said.

Roxborough moved to the nearest heavy bag, nudging the fighter working it out of the way with a gesture. The fighter stepped back, watching.

"Go ahead," Roxborough said.

Joe looked at the bag. It was old; the leather cracked at the seams, the chain above it dark with grease.

"I don't wanna break it," he said.

Roxborough smiled. "You won't break it."

Joe looked at the bag again. "If I do, who pays for it?"

Roxborough laughed. It was his real laugh again, the unpolished one. "I'll pay for it. Hit it as hard and as fast as you can until I tell you to stop."

Joe considered this. Then he shrugged.

He turned to the bag and hit it.

The sound was different from the first blow. It wasn't the deep thud the other fighters made but something harder, flatter, a sound that did not belong in a gym. Joe hit it again. And again. His fists were a blur, his right hand and his left working in alternating arcs, the bag swinging wildly and coming back and getting hit again before it could settle.

The seams of the bag began to fail.

Stuffing came out of the first split slowly, at first, then faster as the bag continued to absorb punishment it had not been designed to absorb. The chain rattled and strained. Fighters across the gym stopped what they were doing. The speed bag went silent. The jump rope stopped whirring. One by one, the sounds of the gym died until there was only the explosive crack of Joe's fists and the deteriorating bag and the chain.

Then the bag came apart.

Stuffing rained down on the floor around Joe. It caught in the hair of the nearest fighters and settled on the canvas of the ring, and drifted across the floor in the draft from the open door. Joe stood with his hands at his sides, breathing evenly. What little was left of the bag swayed on its chain, trailing horsehair.

"That's enough," Roxborough said.

Joe's right hand hung at his side, the knuckles unmarked. Forty years from now, an old man would sit in a hotel suite in Las Vegas and study those same knuckles, gnarled and swollen, but on this afternoon in Detroit, they were young and unbroken, and they had just ended a heavy bag's working life in less than 30 seconds.

The gym was completely still.

Chappie's mouth was open. He closed it. Then opened it again. He looked at the remnants of the bag. He looked at Joe. He looked at Roxborough with an expression that said several things at once, none of them requiring words.

Roxborough looked at the assembled fighters, all of them staring.

"Nobody saw nothing," he said. "Back to work."

He turned to Joe. "Come with me."

The private office was small and smelled of cigar smoke. A desk, three chairs, and a framed photograph of Jack Johnson on the wall. Johnson was the former heavyweight champion of the world and the last black man to hold the title, the man the white boxing establishment had spent years conspiring to bring down. Johnson stared out of the photograph with the expression of a man who was aware of exactly what was being done to him, knew who had the real power, and defied them anyway.

The three of them settled into the chairs. Roxborough leaned forward with his elbows on the desk.

"Joe," he said. "I'm going to make you a rich, rich man. The heavyweight champion of the entire world."

Joe said, "No, thank you."

Roxborough blinked. Whatever he had been prepared for, it was not this. "But why? Why wouldn't you want that?"

"Because I don't want to hurt anybody," Joe said.

Roxborough stared at him. He looked at Chappie. Chappie looked at the wall.

"But that's the sport, Joe," Roxborough said. "They'll be trying to hurt you."

"That don't make it right," Joe said.

Chappie leaned forward. His voice was low and dry, a voice stripped of everything unnecessary. "Way you punch, you can go easy on 'em."

Roxborough seized on it. "That's right. Hell, you just hit 'em in the shoulders, and they'll go down."

"Yeah," Chappie said.

Joe shook his head.

Roxborough shifted in his chair. Joe watched him think, watched him work through his inventory of arguments.

"Joe," Roxborough said. "There has not been a negro heavyweight champ since Jack Johnson. You can become a hero to every black kid in America."

"Sorry," Joe said. "I can't."

He pushed back his chair and started to rise.

"You got a family, right?"

Joe stopped.

Roxborough's voice was quieter now. "Think what all that money can do for them."

Joe stood there with his hands at his sides. He thought about the truck driving north in the red dust. He thought about his mother sitting straight in the passenger seat with her hands folded in her lap, watching the road. He thought about a shit shack on a cotton farmer's land that had never been theirs.

"My Mama wouldn't like it," he said.

Roxborough leaned back in his chair. A slow smile spread across his face.

"I'm pretty sure," Roxborough said, "I can get Mom on our side."

Chapter 3

John Roxborough had charmed his way into a great many living rooms and had talked his way past suspicious mothers, skeptical fathers, and older brothers who answered the door with their arms already crossed. He was a big man in a fine suit, and he knew exactly what he was doing with both. Charm was a tool, the same as money, and he wielded it with the easy confidence of a man who had never once been shown the door before he was ready to leave.

He had not met Lillie Barrow.

She came at him from the far side of the small living room like a weather front. Roxborough stood his ground, or tried to, but the ground had a way of shifting under him every time she opened her mouth.

"You smooth talkin', pimp dressin' jive-ass con man come in here talkin' about how you're gonna help my son!"

Roxborough's smile went somewhere. He was not entirely sure where.

"You're here to help one person only. You. You're gonna make yourself a pile of money off my boy's blood, sweat, and tears!"

From the armchair in the far corner, Munroe Barrow watched all of this over the rim of a beer bottle with the quiet, private satisfaction of a man watching a brush fire about to burn his boss's work truck. He had warned Roxborough, or tried to, but Roxborough had waved him off. Now Munroe tipped the bottle again and laughed softly to himself and kept his opinion where it was safest, which was entirely inside his own head.

"Ma'am, with all due respect —"

"Respect?" Lillie said. The word came out wrong, was turned over, examined, found wanting. "You don't know the meaning of the word."

"I promise you, I got only your son's best interests at heart."

"Shut up."

The two words were not loud. They did not need to be. Roxborough shut up.

"There's only one person I'm interested in hearing from. That's you, Joe."

She turned to her son, and the room turned with her. Joe stood near the window. He felt the full weight of her attention settle on him. It was just his mother, watching him the way she had always watched him.

"Joe," she said, "nobody ever becomes great at nothing unless they really want it and are willing to work hard for it. Now, do you want this?"

The room was very quiet. Outside, somewhere down the block, a car horn sounded and then stopped. Joe could feel Roxborough watching him. He could feel Munroe watching him. He could feel his mother watching him.

"Yes, Mama," he said. "I do."

"Hot damn!"

Munroe Barrow launched himself out of the armchair with a velocity that a man his age had no business producing. He threw a right hand at nothing, then a left, then shuffled his feet on the linoleum. Lillie turned the full force of her attention on him like a searchlight.

"You sit back down. We ain't done here."

Munroe sat down. The beer bottle found his hand again.

Lillie turned back to Joe, and the iron in her voice went in the same direction.

"I don't like the idea of a son of mine making a living with his fists," she said. "But I won't stop you if that's what you want."

Roxborough's smile began its cautious return to his face. Lillie's eyes found him, and it retreated.

"Provided," she said, "you don't match him up in class 'til he's ready. I don't want to see my baby gettin' hurt. He's delicate."

The smile collapsed entirely.

"Delicate?!"

"You heard me."

"Yes, ma'am."

"And if you cheat him outta one thin dime..." Lillie paused, and in that pause was everything a man needed to know about the distance between a legal threat and a personal one. "You ain't gonna have no lawyers suing you. It's gonna be me knocking on your door. You take my meaning?"

"Yes, ma'am."

Lillie nodded. The nod was a gavel.

"All right, Joe. If it's what you want."

Joe looked at her and saw the lines around her eyes that the cotton fields had put there and that Detroit would never take away.

"All I want," he said, "is to make you proud, Mama."

* * *

What followed was not a single moment but a thousand of them, accumulating like sediment.

There was the gym. The smell of it before anything else, the compound of canvas and leather and old sweat and liniment that hit Joe the first morning and never quite left his memory afterward. Chappie Blackburn always had the gym open at five, before anyone else arrived, and Joe was there before Chappie, sitting on the steps in the dark, hands loose between his knees, watching the street wake up around him.

Chappie looked at him for a long moment when he unlocked the door.

"You know what you're doing here?" Chappie asked.

"No," Joe said.

"Good," Chappie said. "A man who thinks he knows what he's doing can't be taught nothing."

The heavy bags were replaced one by one in the first month. The speed bag stayed because Joe went to it gently, learning the rhythm, the counter-intuitive patience it required. Hit too hard, and the thing bucked wildly, gave you nothing, and then laughed at you. Go easy, find the beat, and it sang. He understood this without being told. He understood most things without being told, which was part of what made Chappie watch him as carefully as he did.

The right hand was the thing. It was always the right hand.

Chappie taped it before every session himself, personally, which he did not do for any of the other fighters. He wrapped the knuckles slowly, working between each finger, the gauze tight without being punishing. It was like something sacred was being prepared.

"You feel that?" Chappie would ask.

"Feel what?"

"The difference. Between taped and not."

Joe would flex his fingers inside the wrapping. "Yeah... Like dressing for church," he said.

Joe went easy on the other fighters. He learned early that he could not let himself go. He lived in a different country from what ordinary men did, and the ordinary men around him could not follow him there. So, he calibrated. He learned the dial. He learned to give seventy percent and make it look like everything he had, which was its own kind of skill, maybe harder than any of the rest of it.

The record climbed. Jack Kracken went down in the third. Patsy Perroni in the second. Primo Carnera, the Ambling Alp, six foot six, two hundred and sixty-five pounds of Italian mountain, went down in six rounds and did not seem to understand what had hit him.

Roxborough framed the newspaper clippings. He couldn't help himself.

The numbers rolled upward: 1-0, 6-0, 14-0, 22-0. In the streets of Black Bottom, people called Joe's name as he passed, and he touched the brim of his hat and kept walking, uncomfortable with it in a way he couldn't articulate. He felt like a man who got up early and worked hard and happened to be able to do something other men couldn't, and he was not sure that deserved all the love people were giving him.

The house came on a Tuesday in November. Joe had picked it out without telling anyone. It was in a quieter neighborhood, with a proper yard, with rooms that did not share walls with the neighbors' arguments. He walked his mother up to the front door with his hands over her eyes, and she said, "Joe Louis Barrow, if you make me trip on these steps I will —"

"I got you, Mama," and opened the door and walked her

inside and took his hands away.

She stood in the front hallway and looked at the light coming through the windows, and did not say anything for a long time.

"Well," she finally said.

"Well," he agreed.

She turned and looked at him, this woman who had carried copperheads out of bedrooms and waded into swamp water and stared down lynch mobs, and put John Roxborough in his place without raising her voice above conversational. She looked at her son, at the knuckles of his right hand where he held the keys to the beautiful home, then at something behind his eyes that was still the baby in the crib.

"You always make me proud," she said.

* * *

The arena smelled the way boxing arenas always smell. It was a stale odor of tobacco smoke and the faint, metallic undercurrent of adrenaline that collected in the rafters and never fully dissipated.

Joe sat ringside in a suit that had cost him more than three months of ice route wages and tried to watch the fight with the detached professionalism that Chappie had been drilling into him for two years. Assess. Learn. Observe the tendencies.

The man in the ring was Max Schmeling.

He was the white German counterpart of what Joe was becoming. That was the word going around, the comparison being drawn in sports pages north and south, by writers who meant it as a compliment to Schmeling and something more complicated toward Joe. Watching him was like watching a machine that had been designed to do exactly one thing and had been doing it without deviation or mercy since the day it was switched on.

Schmeling's opponent was trying to clinch. He had been trying to clinch for the better part of three rounds. The clinch was the only safe place in the ring. This fighter was not a fool. He was scared to death. He knew that victory was out of the question and that simple survival was the ultimate goal.

Schmeling looked over the man's shoulder while they were pressed together in the clinch, his eyes moving through the crowd the way a searchlight moves, methodical and unhurried, until they found Joe.

He smiled.

"You're the one I vant, Joe."

Joe said nothing. Beside him, Chappie said it for him.

"Don't pay him no mind."

But Schmeling was not done.

"You vant to see vat I do to you, Joe?"

Schmeling pushed the man back, then the punches that followed were very fast and very heavy, and the last of them sent the man over the top rope. He landed at Joe's feet in a way that left no ambiguity about whether he was conscious.

Joe looked down at him. Looked up at Schmeling, who had his hands in the air and the smile still on his face. The referee was counting. The doctors were moving. The PA announcer said what the crowd already knew.

"The winner by third-round knockout, from Germany, the Black Uhlan of the Rhine, Max Schmeling."

The fallen man lay still. One of the doctors was at his neck, two fingers pressed there, checking. Joe watched this with a stillness. The man's eyes were open but empty.

Schmeling came to the edge of the ring above Joe, looking down.

"Kommen zie hier, Schwartze. Come, fight me now."

Joe rose. It was not a considered decision. His body made it before his mind had a say. But Chappie's hand was already on his shoulder, pressing down.

"You're a pro. You don't fight for free."

Joe looked at the man at his feet again. He was coming to, slowly; his eyes finding focus. Joe felt something cold move through him. The fear arrived the way cold air does: underneath the door, at the edges, before you've acknowledged it was coming.

Max Schmeling watched him, read it, and smiled wider.

"That's okay, Joe. Ven I am champion, you can't hide from me. No one vill protect you."

* * *

The Boxing Commission's office existed in permanent, institutional twilight. The light here was always the color of a headache. The overhead fixtures contributed almost nothing. Everything depended on the amber glow of the table lamps and the aggregate effect of the cigar smoke.

The Commissioner had the look of a man who had spent his career making decisions that other men would have to live with, and who had developed a constitutional inability to accept that any of those decisions might turn out to be wrong.

"It was supposed to be Schmeling-Baer," he said.

"Yeah, but Braddock queered that when he licked Baer." The Assistant Commissioner had the tonal flatness of someone reciting a grievance for the fourth time.

"That wasn't supposed to happen! Christ!"

"That's boxing, chief."

"Bullshit is what it is. Baer had a chance against that Kraut Schmeling, but Braddock? Forget about it."

"It's Schmeling's bout. Nothing we can do about it."

The voice from the back of the room was not loud. It did not need to be. It had the quality of a voice that was accustomed to being the one that ended conversations rather than extended them.

"Schmeling never gets that fight."

The silhouette moved into the light. He was not a large man, but he had the density of someone who had spent a long time being taken seriously by people who were difficult to impress.

The Assistant Commissioner said, "Who the hell are you?"

The Commissioner said, "That's Wild Bill Donovan."

"I work for the president," Donovan said. He set a copy of the New York Times on the table, and the headline — NAZI PLANES BOMB SPANISH VILLAGE. "A Nazi will not become the heavyweight champion of the world."

"But he's next in line."

"He doesn't get the Braddock bout."

The Commissioner found himself in the unusual position of knowing he was no longer in charge of his own meeting. "Who then?"

"Joe Louis."

The silence that followed had several layers.

"Are you serious?!" the Commissioner's voice climbed. "A negro?! That's worse than a Nazi."

Donovan looked at him for a long moment. The look had a quality of filing something away for later.

"I'm gonna pretend I didn't hear that, Commissioner."

He let the pretense hang in the air for exactly as long as it took the Commissioner to understand that it was not a pretense at all.

"Joe Louis gets the fight." He waited for those words to settle into fact. "Now you, me, and the president are all on the same page. Am I right?"

The Commissioner nodded.

* * *

Comiskey Park, Chicago.

The outdoor stadium held forty-five thousand people, and all of them were loud. The night was warm, and the air above the ring shimmered with the blur-strobe of the lights and the compressed body heat of the crowd. Somewhere in the upper deck, a man was ringing a cowbell.

It was not a beautiful fight.

Braddock was careful and disciplined. Joe was somewhere else. Not in the ring. He was at ringside, essentially, because that was where Max Schmeling was sitting in his suit and tie with a Gestapo-looking type in a black leather coat beside him. Schmeling was talking to Joe across the noise of the crowd.

"This was supposed to be my fight, Schwartze! My championship!"

Joe heard it. He heard everything. He heard Schmeling mock him. He heard Braddock breathing in the rhythm of a man who was tired and scared but resolute. He heard the cowbell, distantly, and the roar of 45,000 fight fans.

What he should not have done was lose his concentration.

Braddock came in while Joe was watching Schmeling's mouth move. The right hand was short and accurate, and Joe felt the canvas come up toward him faster than seemed reasonable. He went down on one knee. Less hurt than off-balance, less off-balance than distracted.

"Louis is down!"

The crowd was stunned to near silence. Schmeling leaned forward at ringside and started slapping the mat, counting fast in German.

"Ein, zwei, drei! —"

Joe scrambled to his feet. He could hear Schmeling's derisive laughter; that mocking, rolling laughter that found its way deep into his chest.

Braddock came forward, and Joe clinched with him and pressed his face close and breathed and tried to remember who he was really fighting. The stress of it showed in his jaw, in the tendons of his neck.

Then he glanced at his mother.

Lillie Barrow sat in the front row with her hands in her lap. She saw Joe looking at her, and something moved across her face. It was a micro-expression, there and gone, and Joe knew what it meant. He had been reading her face his whole life.

Then Max Schmeling was at the ropes beside her, looking down at her with that same smile he had been wearing all night, the arrogant smile of a man who believed he had a copyright on the future.

"Is this your mama, Joe? That kind of ugly must run in a family."

Lillie Barrow hit him.

It was an open-handed shot to the side of the face, and it was not tentative. Schmeling's head moved. He brought his hand up to his cheek and looked at her with something that was not quite surprise. And then the smile came back.

"My boy is beautiful," Lillie said.

"She hits harder than you," Schmeling said, and then he turned to Lillie and whispered, "I am going to tear your son's heart out."

Joe heard it. Schmeling intended for him to hear it. The cold anger ran deep into Joe's soul. He let it out in the only way he could at the moment. On Braddock. He was going to show Schmeling what was in store for him.

Joe broke the clinch.

He threw a left. It was followed by a thunderous right, and Braddock went down hard, and the referee's count was merely ceremonial.

Joe went to the ropes. He looked down at Schmeling.

"Schmeling, get in this ring so's I can kill you!"

Schmeling was already moving. He was over the barrier and halfway to the ring before the man in the black coat caught his arm and said something close to his ear, something that stopped him. It was not fear, because Schmeling did not appear to have any. It was something more pragmatic. Calculation.

"I don't kill you now, Joe." Schmeling settled back, straight ening his jacket, the smile returning in a different key. "I let you live a little longer."

Chappie and Roxborough were in the ring, raising Joe's hands, and the noise of the crowd was enormous and immediate and very close.

"Great fight, Champ!" Roxborough exclaimed.

Joe heard it. Processed it. Let the word work on him for a moment. The word *Champ.* The title was his now.

He looked across the ring at Braddock, who was still on the canvas, with the doctors and his corner gathered around him. Joe moved through the celebration toward him, working through the bodies, until he was close.

"I hope I didn't hurt him too bad."

Braddock's eyes focused. He was coming back slowly. He blinked. Swallowed.

Braddock's manager looked up from his crouch. "He'll be okay. You fought a good, clean fight, Joe."

Joe nodded. Then, he pointed across at Schmeling, who was being guided away by the man in the black coat.

"You're next, Schmeling."

Schmeling laughed. He walked away without turning around, which was either contempt or acknowledgment, or both.

Joe stood in the ring while the crowd went on and on around him. He did not entirely know what to do with himself, which was how he usually felt after a fight. Too much sensation, too much noise, no place for any of it to go. He was the champion of the world. He tried to feel the size of that.

He turned to find Roxborough still talking, Chappie's hand on his shoulder, the crowd surging against the ring apron below him.

And at the back of the arena, standing apart from the surge and the noise and the cigarette smoke and the flashbulbs, standing in the same quality of stillness that he had inhabited at the edge of an Alabama swamp fourteen years before, watching a seven-year-old boy ride a gator to the muddy bottom of a river, was the bald white man.

He had seen every moment of the fight.

He turned his collar up and was gone.

Chapter 4

Hollywood, California.

The makeup was the color of old paper, and it sat badly on his skin. Joe felt foolish from the moment the woman in the makeup chair had started applying it, working it over his face with a sponge while he sat still and looked at himself in the mirror and thought about what was happening to him, but decided not to say anything about it. He was the heavyweight champion of the world. He was wearing a white mask in a movie studio in Hollywood, California. He figured if they didn't tell him how to fight, he wouldn't tell them how to make movies.

The scene was simple enough. He sat on a couch opposite an actress who was playing his mother, and he was supposed to tell her he wanted to turn pro. He had lived this moment. He knew every word of it from the inside. The problem was that knowing something from the inside and performing it in front of a camera were entirely different operations, and the version of Joe that lived in front of cameras was a version he did not recognize and did not much like.

He looked straight ahead. He spoke.

"I been talking to a big fight manager, Mama. He wants me to turn pro, and I think it's a good idea."

The words came out stiff and unnatural. The actress opposite him had none of Lillie Barrow's iron. She had a pleasant face and a pleasing manner, and she was entirely wrong for the part. She was what white studio bosses wanted from a black woman. She was meek. Joe thought about Lillie watching this someday and what she would think.

The actress said her lines. Joe said his. An awkward pause opened up at the end of the scene like a hole in the floor, and nobody quite knew what to do with it.

"Cut! Print that."

Harry Fraser came toward him across the studio floor. He was a white man of middle age who had directed enough low-budget pictures to have acquired the habit of moving through sets as though everything there belonged to him, which, in a practical sense, it did.

"Mister Fraser," Joe said, "I think I can do it better."

Fraser smiled.

"No, that was just fine, Joe."

He turned away before Joe could respond.

"Move to the next setup."

The crew moved. They were all white, Joe noticed again, though he had noticed it the first day and every day since. The cast was nearly all black.

Fraser came back toward him with the air of a man performing a courtesy.

"How are you enjoying Hollywood, champ?"

"It's fine."

"Staying out of trouble?"

"Yes, sir."

Fraser reached out and patted him on the head. Joe felt every nerve in his body register it. He was the heavyweight champion of the world. He let it slide. This was not a battle, and Fraser was not worth what winning it would cost. Joe knew the difference between battles and what Chappie would have called noise. He let Fraser walk away, believing the gesture had been received as it was intended.

* * *

The sun was low and orange when Joe walked out of the soundstage at the end of the day, the makeup scrubbed off, his regular face returned to him. He moved along the row of soundstages with his jacket over one arm, in no particular hurry.

He heard the music before he saw the open door.

It was coming from the gap between two large sliding panels, one of which had been left ajar. Sweet, clean music from a live orchestra called out to him.

He went inside to have a look.

A woman was skating. She moved across a sheet of ice that should not exist inside a building in California, and yet here it was, and here she was. The movie crew and the lights and the banks of equipment that surrounded her had somehow faded into the periphery until there was only the single spotlight on her and the music and the way she moved through both of them.

Joe stood in the doorway and watched.

She moved as if she had been designed for exactly this purpose and nothing else. Like every limb was organized around the act of turning and lifting and landing and turning again. He had felt something like this watching great fighters. The economy of it. The way real mastery looked effortless, not because it was easy, but because the person doing it had become an artist.

He watched until the music stopped and the crew moved in

around her, and then he walked on.

* * *

The Beverly Hills mansion sat behind a long drive lined with palms and was lit from outside so that it glowed against the dark California sky.

Roxborough had put on his finest suit for the occasion, which was saying something. He moved through the front rooms with the ease of a man who had been to places like this before, which he had not, but he was not going to let that be apparent to anyone.

Joe moved with him and tried not to look out of place, though he certainly felt it.

There was a great deal to look at. The room was full of people who had arranged themselves into attitudes of casual magnificence. The champagne was flowing at nine o'clock in the evening, and in the corner, a small jazz combo was working through something sophisticated. Joe and Roxborough were the only black faces in the room, save for the waiters, and yet somehow nobody seemed especially troubled by this, which made Joe feel even more nervous because it was unexpected.

"This ain't nothing like Detroit," Joe said.

"No, it isn't." Roxborough accepted a glass from a passing tray. "Have fun, but watch yourself. You know the rules."

"Never get my picture taken with a white woman."

"That's right. You know what happened to Jack Johnson."

Joe nodded. He did know. Every black fighter in America knew what happened to Jack Johnson. It was the cautionary tale that lived underneath every other cautionary tale, the one that went: here is what happens when you forget what country you are in.

You get maliciously prosecuted on trumped-up charges. You have to live much of your life in exile, always on the run.

Joe looked at the room again. Clark Gable was standing near the fireplace, talking to someone Joe recognized but couldn't name. He was about to start counting the faces he'd seen before.

Then he saw the ice skater.

She had come in from somewhere to his left, and she was wearing a dress that was spectacular. She was talking to Clark Gable now, and Joe watched her the way he had watched her through the soundstage door. With the same stillness. The same attention.

"Who's that?"

"Sonja Henie," Roxborough said. "The figure skater and movie star."

"Hot damn."

Roxborough caught the direction of Joe's attention and the quality of it.

"You watch yourself, boy."

"Ha." Joe did not look away. "With all the movie stars around here, she wouldn't be interested in me."

He watched her say something to Gable that made Gable laugh. Then she was moving away from him and across the room. Roxborough appeared to have found something interesting that took him in a different direction.

Sonja Henie stopped in front of Joe Louis and looked up at him with the direct, unafraid quality of someone who did not have a category for intimidation.

"Hello, champ. Can you have a drink, or are you in training?"

"I have a couple weeks off."

She smiled and turned toward the bar, and Joe followed, because there was nothing else to do and also because he wanted to.

"Bobby, two Linie Aquavits, please."

The bartender reached under the bar for a bottle and poured from it into two small glasses. The liquid was clear. The bottle was distinctive. Joe picked up his glass and looked at it.

"Mr. Warner always keeps a bottle for me," Sonja said.

Joe drank. It was unlike anything he had tasted. It went down smooth and came back warm, with something herbal underneath it. He turned the glass in his hand and thought about it.

"Do you like it?" Sonja asked.

"Well, I never tasted nothing like it for sure."

She laughed. The laugh was genuine. He hadn't expected that.

"You don't sound like you're from around here," Joe said.

"Neither do you."

"No, ma'am."

"I'm from Norway. How 'bout you?"

"Detroit by way of Alabama. I'm just in town to make this little movie. It's kinda stupid, really."

"I make movies too," she said. "They're all stupid."

"Yes, ma'am."

"Call me Sonja."

"Yes, ma'am." He paused. The glass was still in his hand, and the Aquavit was still warm in his chest, and he was standing close enough to this woman to be aware of the way she breathed. "I, uh, don't mean to be forward, but you're about the most beautiful white woman I ever seen."

Sonja looked at him. Not at his face exactly. At him. As though she were looking at something she had been trying to locate for a while and had just found in an unexpected place.

"And you're about the most beautiful man I've ever seen."

He smiled. He could feel himself smiling and could not entirely stop it. She put her hand on his arm, and the touch traveled through the fabric of his jacket, and he became suddenly aware of how many people were in this room.

"Ma'am," he said carefully. "Sonja. I don't know how it is in Norway, but here in America, well, my color and yours don't mix so good."

"This isn't America, Joe. It's Hollywood."

He smiled at that. He almost went with it. It was a good line, and she believed it, and part of him wanted to believe it, too. But he had been in enough rooms to know that Hollywood was still inside America, no matter what people here liked to tell themselves.

"Well, good evening to you, ma'am."

He set down the glass and walked back toward the party. He found a quiet corner of the room, saw the garden, and went outside alone. The night air was cool on his face, and the palms made their slow shapes against the sky.

He sat down on a stone bench and listened to the music floating out from inside. The combo had shifted to something slower. Sadder. A song about dancing in the face of bad news. He let it wash over him and looked up at the California stars and thought about Lillie Barrow, and about the new house he had bought for her, and about the right hand he had used to give her the keys.

The night air smelled of flowers. Everything in California smelled like flowers. Detroit smelled like steel and river and whatever dead fish smell came off Lake Erie in November. Alabama smelled like red dirt and pine and the standing water in the low fields.

He thought about Max Schmeling and the match that everyone knew was coming. He thought about what it was going to feel like to stand across from Schmeling with the weight of the title in the arena between them. He flexed the fingers of his right hand in the dark and felt the familiar stiffness in the knuckles and listened to the music.

"Why do you sit out here all alone, Joe?"

He looked up. She was standing there in the garden with the light from the windows behind her, her expression carrying genuine curiosity and no trace of performance. She had followed him. Part of him—a very significant part — hoped that she would join him.

"You, uh, you ever hear of Jack Johnson?" He waited. She shook her head slowly. "Well, he was the last black man to be champ. He got himself involved with a white woman, and well... it didn't turn out good for him. People hated him. Black people and white people."

Sonja was quiet for a moment as the music came through the windows.

"So, you'd rather I left you alone?"

"No ma'am. I just wish the color of our skin didn't matter."

She looked at him for a long time. The garden was dark except for the light from the house windows, and in that light her face was very clear and very serious.

"It doesn't matter," she said. "To me."

The music inside shifted into something too bewitching to ignore. She held out her hand.

"Will you dance with me?"

Joe looked at the hand. Small, certain, extended toward him in the dark garden of a mansion in Beverly Hills while the party went on inside and California did what California did, which was to pretend none of the things that mattered in the rest of the world actually mattered here.

He looked at her face.

He took the hand. He stood. She moved into his arms the way she moved on ice, with no wasted motion, and they were dancing on the dark grass. The garden was very quiet around them except for the music and the distant sounds of the party. Still, they seemed alone.

He thought about Roxborough's rules. He thought about Jack Johnson. He thought about all the reasons this was a thing he should not be doing, and then the song went on, and he stopped thinking about those things. Though they were all true, something much more powerful had taken him over.

Neither of them noticed the bald man in the lit window above, standing with his hands in his pockets, watching everything.

* * *

The name was Weegee. He was famous in certain New York circles for showing up wherever something was happening and pointing a camera at it, and he had a gift for arriving at the precise moment when the thing he was photographing became something other than what it appeared to be. Tonight, he had positioned himself outside a bungalow at the Beverly Hills Hotel, in the shadows near the window where the diaphanous curtains moved with a gentle breeze.

Through the lens, in the warm light of the room, Joe Louis and Sonja Henie were making love.

Weegee shot what he needed. Then he moved away through the dark garden toward the parking lot, the camera against his chest, his footsteps quiet. He had gotten the pictures. He would be back in New York by Tuesday. He allowed himself to feel professional satisfaction.

Two large men stepped out of the shadows.

They were wearing black suits and ties. They had the look of men who were paid to stand in shadows and step out of them at the right moment, and they were very good at their jobs.

"You're a long way from New York, Weegee."

"Yeah." He kept his voice level. "I'm looking forward to getting back there."

The first man hit him in the face. Weegee went down. He was aware of the camera leaving his hands, and he reached for it and missed. The second man caught it on the way up, opened the back, and exposed the film.

"Hey, you can't do that."

"Course we can't." The first man looked at his partner. "See if he's got any more film on him."

"I only shot one roll."

The second man went through his pockets with a thoroughness that left no room for modesty and came out with two more rolls. He put them in his jacket.

"Who hired you?"

Weegee looked up at the first man from his position on the asphalt and made a calculation.

"I suppose you're gonna beat the shit out of me until I tell you."

"That's right."

"Then I'll save you the trouble. I honestly don't know. I got called to a meet in Central Park. I never even saw the guy's face or got a name. He handed me a train ticket and told me to come out here and get pictures of the champ. You know, 'candid' type pictures. Honest, guys."

The two large men looked at each other. They looked back at Weegee.

"We believe you, Weegee."

He got up carefully and tested his face with his fingers and found the damage manageable.

"You're taking pictures for the Nazis, you dupe," the second man said.

Weegee stopped.

"What? I'm a Jew. I wouldn't work for them."

"You just did."

"Don't do it again," the other man said.

They started away. Weegee watched them go and then said, at their backs: "You coulda just told me that. You didn't have to hit me."

The first man turned his head slightly without stopping.

"No problem. I liked hitting you."

* * *

The champagne was open, and the caviar was on the tray, and the robes were the kind of hotel robes that made you understand why people paid this much for a room. Joe lay on his back on the bed and looked at the ceiling, and felt the pleasurable tiredness of a man who had spent himself completely. Sonja was beside him, very much awake.

The bungalow was its own small world. Curtains moved at the window. Champagne sat in the bucket, slowly warming. The ceiling was high and white, and Joe looked at it and thought about the fact that this room cost more per night than a month of ice route wages, and that he had come a considerable distance from hauling hundred-pound blocks up six flights of stairs in

Black Bottom. He was proud of it and uneasy at the same time.

Sonja put some caviar on a cracker, took a bite, and looked at him.

"It's delicious, Joe. Try some."

"What is it?"

"Caviar. Fish eggs."

He looked at the tray. He looked at the small, dark pearls on the cracker in her hand. He frowned.

"I think you'll like it," she said.

She took more of the fish eggs and held them on her tongue and looked at him with an expression that had nothing to do with caviar. He leaned in and kissed her.

"I like caviar."

"I like you, Joe."

He lay back and looked at the ceiling again. The curtains moved at the window. The night was quiet outside.

"You are everything I been warned about."

"Good," she said. She laughed. It was the same genuine laugh from the bar, the one without performance in it. He had decided this was the thing he liked most about her. The laugh and the directness behind it, and how she looked at him in a way that required no particular adjustment on her part.

He thought about Roxborough. He thought about the look on Roxborough's face when Sonja had crossed the room toward him at the party, the way Roxborough had suddenly found something else to look at. Roxborough was not a fool. He was far from a fool. He knew exactly what this country was, and that lingered in the back of Joe's mind, through even the most wonderful moments he had ever experienced.

Joe filed this and set it aside.

"I want to see more of you."

"I do, too." She settled back against the pillow. "But filming is almost done, and I have to go back to Europe, and you have a fight with Max Schmeling to train for."

"Come to the fight," Joe said.

"The fight is in New York. Not Hollywood."

"Hollywood ain't the only place where people can have secrets."

She smiled. She was beautiful when she smiled, and she knew it and did not pretend otherwise. Most of the beautiful women Joe had met in his life pretended not to know how lovely they were. She did not bother with that.

"Okie-dokie, you say, right?"

"Uh huh." He reached over and picked up the small glass of Aquavit from the nightstand. He looked at it. The clear liquid. He felt the warmth of it going down. He thought about ordering a bottle to keep somewhere. He thought this was probably not a practical idea. He set the glass down. "Now, I'd like some more of that caviar, please."

Sonja put more caviar on her tongue and looked at him. He kissed her again. Outside, the California night went on without them, which suited Joe just fine.

Chapter 5

Berchtesgaden, Bavaria.

The Kehlsteinhaus sat above the clouds on its peak in the Bavarian Alps. The full moon was out, and it lit the mountain and the fortress with a cool, indifferent light.

Inside, the chandeliers were blazing, and the finest military minds of the Third Reich were wearing their dress uniforms and talking to each other's wives as they all happily anticipated bringing the entire world to war.

Adolf Hitler stood with Eva Braun and accepted the attention of the room as his natural due. He tapped a glass with a fork, and the room went silent.

"My friends, tonight is a great celebration for a great German. Tomorrow, he crosses the sea and goes to New York, where he will defeat the American Schwartze and bring the heavyweight championship back to Germany. He will prove the superiority of the master race. Ladies and gentlemen, I give you Max Schmeling."

The doors opened, and Schmeling entered with Annie Ondra on his arm. She was a movie star, and she moved like one. Schmeling moved like a man who understood that this moment was a kind of theater and had decided to play it well. Hitler was the first to shake his hand. The others followed in the carefully prescribed order.

Hermann Goering positioned himself at Schmeling's elbow with the comfortable authority of a large man who has never had to compete for space.

"How will you beat such a brute, Max?"

Schmeling moved to the center of the room. He assumed a fighting stance, loose and easy, the stance of a man who has thrown the same punches ten thousand times and knows exactly where they go. Hitler slapped his hands onto his thighs with an expression of pure, uncomplicated delight.

"He is a brute and very powerful. Like a wild animal, he is dangerous. But an animal is always defeated by a man of superior intellect and will. I will destroy him for the glory of the Reich."

The room applauded. Schmeling smiled. Annie touched his arm.

Then the applause changed quality. It brightened. Faces turned toward the door as one when she walked in. Even Hitler's face opened into something that was not quite the expression of a head of state.

Sonja Henie had arrived.

Schmeling raised his voice above the welcome.

"Ladies and gentlemen, the star of the ice and screen, the beautiful and elegant Sonja Henie."

She moved through the room with graceful efficiency, always managing the affection of her audience without being consumed by it. She went directly to Hitler, who kissed her hand with courtly formality. The crowd pressed in around her with hugs and the social noise of people who thrilled to witness a high drama that would put the best of Hollywood to shame.

This wasn't staged for the cameras. This was as real as it gets.

Annie Ondra found a moment near Sonja's ear.

"Is Tyrone Power as good a lover as he appears?"

"I don't kiss and tell," Sonja said.

Joseph Goebbels had been waiting. He always waited for the right moment, with the stillness of someone in whom patience had curdled into something else. He had formed his base of power through subtle obsequiousness while he punished those below him. He found his opening and guided Sonja by the elbow toward a quieter corner of the room.

"I've heard you have won the heart of the negro."

Sonja kept her face composed. The thing she felt when he said the word was something she had gotten very good at not showing.

"Yes."

"I hope it wasn't too disturbing."

She said nothing.

"Have you made arrangements to see him before the fight?"

"Yes. Why?"

Goebbels produced a small glass vial from his jacket pocket. The liquid inside was clear. He held it out to her.

"The night before the fight, you will put this in his drink. It will make him sluggish and guarantee Max's victory."

Sonja looked at the vial. She looked at Goebbels.

"If the Aryan race is so superior, why is this drug necessary?"

Goebbels smiled the smile of a man who considers a question like this a sign of charming naivety.

"The Aryan Race *is* superior, but this fight is too important to the Reich to even take a chance that the gorilla could win. The Fuhrer himself stands behind your mission."

She looked across the room at Hitler. He was looking at her.

He had been looking at her since Goebbels had guided her to this corner. His eyes had the quality she had noticed the first time she met him: a flatness behind whatever expression occupied the front of his face, as though the expression were scenery and the real thing was somewhere behind it, looking out. And the real thing always contained some form of cruelty.

Goebbels moved closer.

"I know this is unnecessary, but the Fuhrer wants me to remind you that we have SS men very close to your family's home in Norway."

She took the vial.

Goebbels leaned toward her ear. His breath was warm, and she focused on the chandelier above them and waited for him to finish saying what he was going to say.

"So. Later? In my room?"

"Of course, Herr Goebbels."

She said it cleanly, without a pause, because a pause would have cost her something she was not willing to spend in this room. She swallowed what she felt. She looked across the room at Schmeling, who was still holding court near the fireplace, and then at Hitler, who was still watching her. She held the vial in her closed hand and waited for the evening to be over.

* * *

The private screening room was small and dark, and smelled of leather. Hitler sat in the front row like a man at a picture show, leaning slightly forward, his hands on his knees. The footage on the screen was black and white and grainy, and showed Joe Louis fighting.

Schmeling sat beside him and watched his own analysis take

shape.

"You see it. The jab, and he drops his left arm. Boom, comes my right cross. Down goes Louis. Down goes Louis!"

Hitler slapped his knees with childish delight. This was a man watching something he was certain was going to happen.

"My right hand makes me invincible."

On the screen, Joe Louis moved. Even in the grainy, flickering footage, there was something about the way he moved that the camera could not quite flatten, a quality that survived the translation from three dimensions to two. Schmeling watched it, understood it, and believed he had found the door through it.

* * *

Pompton Lakes, New Jersey. Training Camp.

The sparring partner who stood across from Joe Louis bore a passing resemblance to Max Schmeling in terms of general size and coloring. In terms of everything else, the resemblance broke down quickly, which was why he was a sparring partner rather than a contender. Joe worked methodically, knowing exactly what he was practicing for, and he was not confused about the gap between the practice and the reality of the fight itself.

Boom, boom. He found the sparring partner with a combination and put him down.

Joe came to the ropes. The photographers and sportswriters were banked three deep outside the ring, held back by a rope that everyone understood was a courtesy rather than a barrier. They shouted their questions as if volume were a strategy.

One voice cut through.

"Joe, Max Schmeling says he's got a plan to knock you out."

Joe looked at the sportswriter.

"Everybody got a plan 'til they get punched in the face."

The sportswriters laughed. More questions came up from the noise. A second voice found the gap.

"Max Schmeling claims he can't lose because he has all of Germany in his corner."

Joe unwrapped his right hand from the top rope, where he had been leaning, and considered this.

"I don't know who all is gonna be in his corner, but when he steps into that ring, he's gonna find himself all alone."

More laughter. More questions. A third voice, different in quality from the others, with a pompous disregard for the unwritten rules of this sort of interview. He wanted to make the moment uncomfortable on purpose.

"Adolf Hitler has said that a Negro shouldn't fight for the United States because he's a second-class citizen here."

The camp grew quieter. The laughter was gone.

Joe looked at the sportswriter for a long moment. Then he looked at the assembled group of them, all the faces and all the pencils and all the expectations about what he was going to say and whether he was going to say it quietly or loudly.

"I'll take America over Germany and them Nazis any day. I'm proud to fight for my country."

The sportswriters cheered. They were not always a generous audience, but they were a responsive one, and they understood when a man said something that was going to read well in the morning edition and was also exactly what he meant.

Joe made his way down from the ring. Chappie was at the steps with the towel, and Joe took it and pressed it against his face.

When he took it away, the camp was still going on around him, the noise and the motion of it, but he was already somewhere else, already inside the thing that was coming.

* * *

New York City. The Waldorf Astoria.

The suite was everything a suite at the Waldorf Astoria was supposed to be. The bed was unmade, and there was caviar on a tray, and the robes were thick, and the night outside the window was New York at its most enormous. The city going on in all directions at once.

Joe was not sitting down. He stood, and then he moved to the window, and then he moved back, and then he stood again. The nervous energy had nowhere to go. It was the night before the fight, and his body knew it even when his mind was trying to have a conversation. He had been in this place before, the place where the fight was still future tense and everything in him was already pointed at it, already there, and the hours between now and then were just time to get through.

Sonja watched him from the sofa. She was an athlete and understood. She had the vial in her mind. She had been carrying it since Berchtesgaden, and it had gotten heavier on the crossing and heavier still in New York, and she had not slept well in three nights because whenever she closed her eyes she was back in that corner of the room with Goebbels's breath on her ear and the flatness in Hitler's eyes across the room and the weight of the small glass tube in her closed hand.

She thought about her family's home in Norway. She thought

about SS men she had never seen and would never see, standing somewhere near it.

She thought about Joe.

"Have a drink, Joe. Relax."

"Nothing but water before a fight."

"Then let's go for a walk through town."

"We can't. There's photographers everywhere."

He crossed to the window and looked down at the street. The crowd below saw him and started cheering as they pointed up at him. The sound of it came up through the glass, muffled and enormous.

Sonja reached into her robe pocket. She took out the vial. She looked at the glass of water on the table beside her. She looked at Joe's back, the breadth of it, the way he stood when he was looking at something he was trying to understand.

She poured the contents of the vial into the glass.

Her hand was steady. She had made the decision. Or she had made one version of the decision. She put the empty vial back in her pocket, and picked up her champagne, and was looking at the window when Joe turned from it.

"You are their hero," she said.

"Hero today, lynched tomorrow."

He moved back into the room, away from the glass.

"If they knew you were in here with me, they'd string me up in Central Park."

"Surely not."

"They were gonna lynch my cousin back home just for looking at a white woman the wrong way." He stopped pacing. He stood in the center of the room with his hands at his sides. "'Wrong way?' What does that even mean?"

"But it's not like the South here..."

"Oh, no? Come on over and give me a kiss in front of the window so's they can all see."

She started to rise. He shook his head.

"No. Don't."

"I'm not afraid."

"You should be."

He walked back to her. He sat down. The glass of water was on the table between them, and she was very much aware of it.

"Only reason my country's rooting for me is 'cause I'm all they got against that Nazi."

"That's so sad, Joe."

"It's okay. 'Cause in that ring, all the sad goes away. It's just me and the other guy. And the better boxer wins. It's fair and honest, and it ain't about the color of your skin."

He paused. When he continued, his voice had something in it that was different from the press conference voice, and different from the sparring voice, and different from the voice he used when he was being careful with someone.

"When I fight, I stand tall. And my heart is full. And I'm a man."

Sonja looked at him. She looked at the glass of water on the table. She looked at his face, the face she had watched from across a party in Beverly Hills when he was the only man in the room she wanted to meet.

He reached for the glass.

Her hand shot out and caught it first, and the glass went over, and the water spread across the table and dripped to the floor and was gone. She held the moment together by will. She had submitted enough for one lifetime, and she couldn't do this. She couldn't destroy a man she loved, no matter the cost.

"I'm sorry. I'll pour you another one."

She took the pitcher and poured clean water into a fresh glass and handed it to him. He drank it and set it down and looked at the window, and thought about tomorrow.

Outside, the city continued. Inside, she sat with the decision she had made and tried to understand what it was going to cost. The SS men near her family's home were still there. If Joe won the fight, there would be hard consequences.

* * *

Yankee Stadium, New York.

The graphic outside read: JOE LOUIS VS. MAX SCHMELING. HEAVYWEIGHT CHAMPIONSHIP. YANKEE STADIUM.

Then there was no more time for graphics.

The fight was savage. Two men who had been built by different countries and different systems for different purposes finally met in the same ring at the same time without anything between them, and both of them went at it with everything they had.

Seventy thousand people in Yankee Stadium, and the whole thing was in the present tense. The whole thing was right now, no history yet, no outcome, just the two of them and the lights and the noise and the pressure in the chest of everyone in attendance.

Joe worked the jab. He knew about Schmeling's right cross. He had watched the footage and listened to Chappie a thousand times. He knew all about the damned right cross. The knowledge was there. He carried it into every exchange. And Schmeling carried the right cross into every exchange too, probing for the opening that the footage had shown him existed, the moment when Joe's jab fired, and he returned the left arm too low.

Round after round.

Joe's face began accumulating the evidence of the night. A cut opened above his left eye in the fourth round, and the blood was a problem he had to manage on top of everything else. Chappie worked on it between rounds with practiced hands, talking into his ear, low and steady. Joe nodded and went back out.

The big Schmeling right hand found its opening in the twelfth round. Joe knew it was coming. Knowing it was coming and being able to stop it are different things. The canvas arrived fast, and he was on it, and the referee was counting, and seventy thousand people were making that horrible sound.

He got up. He always got up.

The final rounds arrived with both men wearing everything the other one had thrown. Joe's face was not his face anymore. It was a thing that had been worked on extensively by a craftsman using the only tools available, which were Max Schmeling's fists. His eyes were swollen to slits. Blood ran into them from cuts that Chappie had closed on his eyebrows and had opened again. He blinked through it and found Max in his narrowed field of vision and moved toward him because there was nothing else he could do.

Joe fired his left hand. Max threw the right hand over the top of it.

Joe went down and did not get up.

The count echoed through Joe's mind, but seemed hollow and distant. Get up, he thought. But he couldn't. The noise of the stadium was an ocean, and inside it, seventy thousand people processed what they had just seen and were not prepared for.

All of them were now on the other side of the event and figuring out what that meant. Joe Louis had been knocked out.

* * *

The locker room had the stillness of a funeral home before the mourners arrived. Just a mortician and a corpse. Chappie worked Joe's shoulders with his hands. Roxborough sat against the wall with his jacket off and his tie loosened and said nothing. If they had been children, they would have been crying, but they weren't children. They were men, but they were damned close to crying, anyway. Joe sat on the bench with his face buried in his hands and looked at the floor through the gaps between his fingers.

The door opened.

Max Schmeling came in. His face bore the marks of the evening, too. He had not escaped unscathed, and he was not pretending otherwise. He stood in the doorway for a moment and looked at Joe.

"You are a good fighter, Joe. The best to ever stand in the ring with me."

Joe looked up. His face in the light of the locker room was something that required a moment to process. The swelling had closed his eyes to slits. The bruising had changed the geography of his features. He was almost unrecognizable, and he knew it, and it was not the thing he was thinking about.

"How the hell did you ever lose three fights?" Joe asked.

Schmeling considered this.

"Sometimes to lose is better than to win. It makes one seem more menschlich..." He searched for the English. "...human."

"You saying you threw those fights?" Joe asked.

"I am saying only that you are a good fighter," Schmeling answered.

Joe nodded. He understood. He was not sure he agreed with it, but he understood it.

Max looked at him for another moment. The mutual respect in the room was not a comfortable thing. It was the kind of respect that exists between two people who have just tried very hard to destroy each other and have discovered that the other one is harder to destroy than expected. It does not make anyone feel good. It does make everyone feel honest.

"What do they do to make you so strong?"

"Huh?"

Max looked at Joe's confusion and saw that the question had not landed the way he intended it. He moved past it.

"Never mind... You are a great fighter."

"Not great enough, I guess."

"I think maybe ve do this again."

Max tapped him on the top of the head with one hand, lightly, the gesture of a man acknowledging something he cannot quite put into words, and then he left. The door closed behind him. Joe looked at the floor. His hands were in his lap, the right hand visible, the knuckles swollen as they always were after a fight. He did not look at his hand. He looked at the floor.

Nobody said anything for a long time.

* * *

The limousine moved through the New York night. Joe sat in the back with his sunglasses on and his hat pulled low, and looked at nothing but the passing lights and the reflection they made in the windows.

Roxborough cleared his throat.

"How you feeling, champ?"

Joe turned and looked at him from behind the sunglasses. The look was not complicated, but it was complete. Roxborough heard what it said.

"Sorry, Joe..."

"I just wanna get home."

"I hear you. Get home and re-group, right?"

Joe looked out the window at the city passing by. The city did not look back. It had its own concerns.

The limousine pulled to a stop outside Grand Central Station. Joe got out. He moved through the main concourse with his hat down and his sunglasses on and his coat collar up, and he was not, probably, going to be recognized. He needed to not be recognized tonight above almost any other consideration he could think of.

The concourse was enormous around him. Grand Central at night was an entire universe. The vaulted ceiling above and the constellations painted on it in green and gold, and the thousands of people moving through it in all directions, everyone with a destination that mattered to them. Joe moved through it toward his terminal and did not look at anyone.

He did not look behind him.

If he had looked behind him, he would have seen the two large men in black suits, the ones who had relieved Weegee of his camera in a Beverly Hills parking lot, moving through the crowd twenty feet back, staying with him the way professionals stay with someone.

He was almost at his terminal when a figure stepped out of the crowd in front of him.

The figure was not large. He was a compact man of middle

age with a bald head and the kind of stillness that is acquired.

"Mr. Louis, there's somebody you need to meet," the bald man said.

"Don't want to meet nobody."

Joe moved to go around him. The two large men from the parking lot were suddenly on either side of him, each with a hand on an arm. One of them shifted his jacket in a way that was deliberate and informative. The gun in the holster underneath it was visible for exactly as long as it needed to be.

The bald man looked at him steadily.

"'fraid I'm gonna have to insist."

They moved him down an offshoot hallway that branched from the main concourse, away from the crowd and the noise and the painted constellations on the ceiling above. The bald man walked ahead. His name was Stephen Mercer. He had been watching Joe Louis for sixteen years.

He reached the wall at the end of the hallway. He pressed something. A door opened in the wall where there had not been a door. It was perfectly flush with the surrounding stone, and it opened without a sound. On the other side of it was light.

They hustled Joe through it.

Chapter 6

New York City. Grand Central Station.

The room on the other side of the invisible door was not large, but it was dense with purpose. Maps on the walls. A desk. Filing cabinets. A telephone that looked like it had been modified in ways that were not immediately apparent. Whatever this place was, it had been here for a while.

Joe stood in the center of it, looked at what there was to look at, and tried to understand what had just happened to him. He had walked into Grand Central Station as a man who wanted to go home and had been walked through a wall by three people he had never met, one of whom had a gun he was willing to show.

"What the hell's going on!"

"I know how Schmeling beat you."

Joe turned toward the voice. A man sat at the desk. Joe didn't know who he was, but immediately sensed he was the man who mattered most.

"Right cross," Joe said.

"That's not the half of it."

The man stood and came around the desk.

"I'm Bill Donovan. I work for the U.S. government. OSS."

"I pay my taxes."

Donovan smiled.

"Not the IRS, the OSS. Office of Strategic Services."

He held out a business card. Joe took it and turned it over. Both sides were blank. He frowned at it.

"It doesn't officially exist yet." A moment passed. "Take the glasses off, Joe."

Joe removed the sunglasses. The light in the room found his face and revealed what it looked like to have your features rearranged by Schmeling's fists. It showed everything. The swelling. The discoloration. The geography of the evening was rendered in bruises and cuts.

Mercer, standing to one side, looked at him and made the mistake of thinking this was a moment for levity.

"You look like you just went twelve rounds with Max Schmeling."

Joe's eyes found him. Whatever Mercer saw in them, he took a step back and said nothing further.

"Look, I don't know what you're selling, mister, but I ain't buying."

Joe turned toward the door. One of the large men stepped into his path. Joe hit him once, a short right hand that arrived without announcement, and the man went down. Joe stepped over him and reached for the door.

"Joe, I can have you arrested for miscegenation."

Joe stopped. He did not turn around immediately. He stood with his hand on the door and let the word settle.

Then he turned.

"Miss what?"

"Race mixing. We know all about your relationship with Sonja Henie."

Joe looked at Donovan for a long moment. When he spoke,

his voice was very even.

"You go public with that, I'll miscegenation your face."

"Joe, I don't care about that at all. I'm here because the world is heading for war with Germany. The OSS was created to get us ready for that war, and I run the OSS."

"What's that got to do with me?"

"Your country needs you."

"Not no more. Schmeling beat me."

"That's because he cheats."

Joe frowned. This was not a direction he had expected the conversation to go.

"He's, how to put it?... 'Enhanced.' Created in a lab by Nazi scientists to be a symbol for the master race."

"Man, you lost me," Joe said.

Donovan smiled again.

"We want you to work for us against the Nazis."

Mercer stepped forward, finding his footing again.

"We've been watching you for a long time, and we think there is something very special about you... something that makes you superior to other men in a lot of ways."

"What you talking about?"

"I'm talking about a seven-year-old boy whipping a 500-lb. alligator."

The room went quiet. Joe felt the chill of something he thought was buried being dug up.

"Hey... what's going on here?"

"We want you to be an agent for the US government," Donovan said.

"Like a spy?"

"Better than that. We want you to be our hero against the Krauts. A Fantastic Man, or something like that."

Joe looked at him.

"Fantastic Man?"

"Or Mighty Guy. We haven't got the name worked out."

"We want you to come to DC so we can put you through some tests," Mercer said, "to see exactly what you're capable of."

Joe looked at Donovan. He looked at Mercer. He looked at the man still on the floor by the door, who was beginning to think about getting up.

"Look, man, I'm a Negro, and I know for damn sure this country ain't ready for no 'Mighty Negro.' My mama warned me 'bout that long ago."

"Joe, I'm not a man who sees black and white. I only see red, white, and blue."

"Sorry, but I ain't interested."

Donovan was quiet for a moment. Then he said something that was different in register from everything else he had said. It was not a tactical move, just a man saying what he actually thought.

"Joe, the way your people have been treated in this country makes me ashamed to be a white man. But we got spies on the ground in Germany, and what Hitler and his goons are doing there is worse than anything you can imagine. He gets his way; he'll wipe your entire race off the planet along with a few other races as well."

Joe said nothing. The man by the door had gotten himself to his knees... barely.

"When what you do for us comes out," Donovan said, "it'll change the picture on race relations over the entire world."

Joe stood with Donovan's words surrounding him. He looked at the blank business card still in his hand. He looked at the maps on the wall. He looked at his right hand, the knuckles still swollen from the fight.

He thought about his mother, Lillie Barrow. He thought about what she had said to him earlier in the day, when she had come to his room and looked at what Schmeling had done to his face and had not flinched, because she was Lillie Barrow and flinching was not something she did. She had said: *there are battles that need fighting that you can't always see from where you're standing.* He had thought she meant the rematch. He was no longer sure that was all she meant.

He thought about the alligator. He had not thought about the alligator in years. He had buried it in the same place he buried the copperhead and the lynch mob and all the other things that did not fit into the story of his life as a professional fighter. The man across from him, Stephen Mercer, had been at that river. Had watched a seven-year-old boy do something that seven-year-old boys do not do. Had filed it and waited and followed him for sixteen years through gyms and arenas and Beverly Hills gardens.

He thought about Max Schmeling. About the right hand that had found its opening in the twelfth round. "Enhanced," Donovan had said. Created in a lab by Nazi scientists. Joe had no framework for this, and he knew it, and he set it to one side and focused on what he did have a framework for, which was the feeling of the canvas and the count and losing when he was beginning to think he could not be beaten.

He looked at the blank card again.

He said nothing. But he did not leave.

* * *

Washington, D.C. The Oval Office.

The room smelled of cigars and power. Franklin Delano Roosevelt sat in his wheelchair at the center of it with the bearing of a man who had decided long ago that the chair was not the most important thing about him, and who had largely persuaded the world of this.

J. Edgar Hoover sat to his left with Clyde Tolson arranged at his elbow like punctuation. Donovan and Mercer occupied the other side of the room. A 16-millimeter projector sat on a table, pointed at a screen.

"Over the last several months, we gathered all the 'special' candidates we've been watching over the years," Donovan said, "and subjected them to a series of tests. Which we filmed."

He paused. "Mr. Mercer."

Mercer turned off the lights. Donovan turned on the projector. The machine clattered to life and threw its beam across the room, and on the screen a grainy black-and-white image came to life: Joe Louis and ten other men in bathing suits, standing around a swimming pool.

"The first test was breath-holding in a swimming pool."

Hoover leaned toward Tolson with the practiced ease of a man sharing a joke he has already decided is funny.

"A darkie in a swimming pool. This should be rich."

On the screen, all eleven men jumped into the pool. A large clock beside the pool began ticking.

The footage shifted. Tests of speed. Tests of agility. Dexterity. Strength. The images came in sequence, grainy and matter-of-fact, the camera recording what it saw without comment.

Joe and the other candidates ran down a street. Joe pulled ahead. Joe pulled further ahead. The others fell back and then disappeared from the frame entirely as Joe continued to accelerate. Ahead of him, the camera car sped up to stay ahead of him. Joe ran faster. The car sped up again. Joe caught it. Joe passed it.

"Joe was clocked at 61 miles an hour," Donovan said. "Three times faster than any human being has ever been recorded."

The clock by the pool on screen ticked to three minutes. One of the other candidates surfaced.

Nine men on one side of a thick rope. Joe, on the other side, held his end with one hand, looked at the nine men with an expression of mild interest. The nine men pulled with all their might. Joe yanked once, a short, controlled motion, and the nine men went across the line in a tumble of arms and legs and wounded dignity.

The clock ticked on. Candidates five, six, and seven surfaced from the pool, gasping.

An obstacle course. The other candidates were working their way up a twelve-foot wall with ropes. Joe appeared at the base of the wall, assessed it briefly, and cleared it in one jump, sailing over the heads of the men still climbing.

Candidates eight, nine, and ten surfacing from the pool.

A thick brick wall with a steel-reinforced door. The other candidates worked at the brick with sledgehammers, making slow progress. Joe walked up to the steel door. He reared back and punched it off its hinges.

The swimming pool clock continued ticking. The last candidate burst to the surface at eleven minutes. The clock continued. No Joe.

Fifteen minutes. Twenty. Thirty. Forty-five.

Still no Joe.

"We had an underwater camera," Donovan said, "so we knew

he was still alive."

The underwater footage showed Joe sitting on the bottom of the pool. Eyes closed. Arms loose at his sides. On the floor of a pool, in what appeared to be total comfort.

"Finally, we had to send a diver after him."

A diver plunged into the pool and descended to where Joe sat. The diver shook him. Joe's eyes opened, not with the panicked urgency, but with the slow, disgruntled quality of a man who had been somewhere pleasant and had been interrupted. He swam to the surface.

The clock read 47 minutes.

Mercer turned the lights back on. The projector chattered to a stop.

"Forty-seven minutes," Donovan said. "He might still be down there if we hadn't pulled him out."

Roosevelt leaned forward in his chair.

"But that's physically impossible."

"Not for Joe Louis," Mercer said.

Hoover had been quiet throughout the footage, preparing what he was going to say next.

"So what? He can hold his breath. He's a strong buck."

"Strong buck?" Donovan turned to look at him. "He's a hell of a lot more than that."

"We all know that when the chips are down, you cannot count on the Negro," Hoover said, raising his voice. "It's a well-known fact that they are lazy and have no moral code."

"You're full of shit, Hoover," Donovan shouted back.

Hoover's face did several things in rapid succession.

"Really? So how was it that your black superman was knocked senseless by the German, Max Schmeling? The Negro will always fold."

"Schmeling has been genetically altered by the Nazis."

"You have no proof of that whatsoever."

Roosevelt cleared his throat. It was a quiet sound, but it had the effect of a gavel.

"J. Edgar, whose side are you on here?"

Roosevelt pushed himself to his feet with the effort that his polio always cost him and that he never acknowledged.

"Quite frankly, I'm weary of your flimsy racist ranting."

He turned to Donovan.

"Joe Louis is extraordinary. You have my blessing to go ahead with your plan, Bill."

"You cannot give this position to a Negro." Hoover's voice had climbed past argument into something closer to anguish. "I protest."

"*The lady doth protest too much, methinks*, Mr. Hoover," Donovan said.

"Let's go, Clyde."

Hoover left the room at a speed that was not quite dignified, Tolson at his heels. The door closed behind them. Donovan turned to Roosevelt, who was smiling.

"I've heard he has a little coffee in his cream," Donovan said.

Roosevelt's smile broadened. He said nothing. Some things are funnier left alone.

* * *

Washington, D.C. Beneath the Washington Mall.

They went down a long way. The elevator had no numbers on its panel, only a single button, and when it stopped, and the doors opened. The lab was the size of an airplane hangar. Joe stepped out and looked at what was in it, immediately impressed.

Men were training in martial arts in one corner. Another man attempted to climb upside down on the ceiling using suction cups. He fell while Joe was watching. A man fired an electricity gun at a mannequin, and it caught fire. Strange guns were mounted along one wall, larger artillery in various stages of construction along another. The smell of machine oil and electricity, and the dry smell of static air in a space that has been sealed from the outside world for a long time.

Mercer led Joe through it with the proprietary ease of a man giving a tour of something he helped build. One machine stopped Joe. It was circular, about twelve feet across, with a large screw-top blade assembly mounted above the platform. The design had an old quality to it, as though it had been drawn by someone working from very old plans.

"That thing's supposed to fly?"

"Like a dream," Mercer said. "It's the Da Vinci flier."

They moved on. A long row of secretaries typed with great concentration. Mercer pulled a sheet from the nearest typewriter and held it up. It was blank.

"Secret message department," Mercer said.

Joe nodded slowly.

"You boys got yourself quite an operation here."

"We're coming to the best part."

They turned into a partitioned section of the hangar. Above the entrance, a sign read: MIGHTY GUY DEPARTMENT.

Joe looked at the sign. He shook his head.

"We know we need to change that name," Mercer admitted.

The department contained a row of mannequins, each wearing a different uniform. Joe's eyes moved down the row and stopped on one in particular. Red, white, and blue. Tights. A star on the chest. An area of the uniform in the vicinity of the groin had been arranged with apparent optimism.

Donovan was standing beside it.

"This is where you come in. What do you think, Joe?"

"You serious?"

"We want you to wear it. Red, white, and blue. It makes a very patriotic statement."

Joe looked at the uniform for a moment. He wanted to play ball and accept it, but he just couldn't fake it. Finally, he shook his head.

"Nope. I ain't wearing them sissy britches. Might as well paint a target on my ass."

"But there's a shield, too," Mercer said.

He produced a round shield with a star at its center.

"There's the target right there," Joe said.

"A shield, Joe. With a star. Bullets bounce right off it."

"How am I gonna fight with a shield on my arm?"

Mercer had the exasperated look of a man who has invested considerable effort in a project and is watching it encounter unexpected resistance.

"We've come up with a great name, too."

"What's that?"

"Captain America."

Joe looked at the uniform. He looked at the shield. He looked at Mercer.

"When's the last time you seen a captain wearing tights and carrying a shield?"

A beat.

"Besides, I already got a nickname. The Brown Bomber."

Donovan had been quietly amused as he let the exchange run

its course.

"Has a nice ring to it," Donovan said.

"But sir," Mercer said, "our marketing department says 'Captain America' is perfect."

"We'll go with the Brown Bomber."

Mercer opened his mouth. Donovan's expression closed it.

"What about a uniform, Joe?"

"I like me a nice tailored suit. I'm partial to gabardine. You can be bold with the colors, but not as bold as that Captain fancy tights outfit." He paused. "You gonna pay for that, right?"

Donovan and Mercer looked at each other and nodded.

"And I'm gonna need me some wheels."

"We've got just the thing," Mercer said.

He moved to a curtain at the far end of the department and pulled it open. Behind it sat a vehicle that someone with a great deal of imagination and a very specific aesthetic had apparently spent considerable time on. It was low and black and angular in ways that cars were not yet angular, with wing-like protrusions that suggested either great speed or great instability, or possibly both. It looked like a vehicle from a future that had not entirely decided what it wanted to be.

Joe stared at it for a long moment.

"Oh, hell no. That looks like some kind of bat thing."

"With all due respect," Mercer said, "we've done a lot of research on this before you stepped into the picture."

"Have it your way. But get yourself another 'mighty guy.'"

Mercer turned to Donovan with an expression of appeal. Donovan was already smiling.

"Joe. Your way all the way."

* * *

The Duesenberg was a 1935 Dual Cowl Phaeton SJ in a color that could only be described as the color of money if money had better taste. It was a long car and a beautiful one, and it moved through the New York street lazily, as if saving itself for something more important.

Joe drove it with one hand on the wheel and the window down, and people on the sidewalk turned when he passed, called his name, and waved. He touched the brim of his hat. He kept moving.

He was motivated again. His defeat at the hands of Schmeling was in the past and would be kept there. He was thinking about a bold new future. Revenge against Schmeling would be part of it, but for now, he worked for the United States government in a capacity that did not officially exist. He drove a car that cost more than most men made in five years. He was wearing a gabardine suit in a shade of blue that Donovan's tailor had called French navy.

He had been warned about men like Donovan his whole life. He had been warned about white men who look at black men and see a resource to be developed and deployed, and then set aside when the deployment is complete. Roxborough was not that kind of man, which was why Joe trusted him. Chappie was not that kind of man either. Donovan, he was still reading.

What he could not argue with was his location. He had met the President of the United States and was now working with some of the most important people in the world. Politicians and scientists were deferential to him. When he said "no," they accepted it as the final word.

He had always known there was something different about him. He had known it in the body, and in the moment when you pull your punch in the gym, because you can feel what happens if you don’t. Who he was as a man was all coming into focus for him now. Knowing the why of it wasn’t far away either. It lay across the ocean in Germany, and the inevitability of a war that had not yet begun publicly but was already well underway.

Chapter 7

New York City.

Joe stood before the stone portico of City Hall with Roxborough and Chappie; the press gathered a few steps below them, the questions already starting before anyone had signaled that they could.

"Joe, how you feeling about the rematch with Schmeling?"

"Feeling real good."

"What do you think about the Krauts agreeing to have the fight in New York instead of Germany?"

"Don't matter to me. I'll fight him anywhere, any timc."

The reporters wrote this down and shouted more questions, and Joe let the noise wash over him and answered what he answered and declined what he declined. He gave them Joe Louis, public edition. He kept the rest where it was.

Roxborough stood at his shoulder and said nothing about the Duesenberg parked around the corner. He had significant questions about it, but decided, at least temporarily, to keep it to himself.

Chappie stood on the other side and also said nothing. Chappie was good at saying nothing. It was one of the things Joe valued most about him.

* * *

Berlin. The Reich Chancellery.

The screening room in the Reich Chancellery was smaller than Hitler's private one at Berchtesgaden, but the furniture was finer, which was saying something. The film was the same as always. It was the first fight, the Louis-Schmeling footage that had been watched and rewound and watched again in rooms across two continents by people who had very different feelings about what they were seeing.

Hitler watched it with the focused attention of a man looking for something specific. Goebbels sat to his left. Sonja sat to his right, which was not a comfortable place to be.

"Despite the drugs, the Schwartze was surprisingly effective."

"Yes," Sonja said. "He is not like most men."

Hitler's eyes did not leave the screen.

"He was so effective, it makes me wonder if he was drugged at all."

The room temperature dropped several degrees in the space of a sentence. Sonja felt it on her skin.

"I assure you, my Fuhrer, that I saw him drink the entire contents of the glass."

Hitler turned to look at her. The look had the quality she had noticed the first time she sat in a room with him. It was not the look of a man assessing what you were saying but of a man assessing what you were. As though the words were a distraction from the real examination happening somewhere behind his eyes.

She held it. She was an actress and had learned to hold it. The alternative was worse.

Goebbels stepped carefully into the silence.

"Perhaps we underestimated his power and strength. The negro doesn't react to things the way a normal person would."

Hitler considered this. The film ran on. Joe Louis moving on the screen in the flickering light. Then came Schmeling's knock out punch.

"Yes, perhaps."

He gave Sonja one final look that was not quite an accusation and not quite an absolution. Then he left. The door closed. The film kept running for a moment before Goebbels reached over and stopped it.

The two of them sat in the dark of the room and understood each other without having to say so. He had saved her. They both knew it, and neither of them mentioned it, because that was how these things worked.

"So, I hear you will be going back to Hollywood to shoot a movie."

"Yes. 'Sun Valley Serenade' with John Payne, Glenn Miller, and Milton Berle."

Goebbels had been nodding pleasantly through the list until the last name.

"Why must they always include a Jew?"

He shook his head. He turned to her.

"I suppose they find Jews funny," he said. "Stay close to Louis. And await further orders."

Sonja nodded. She looked at the blank screen where Joe Louis had been moving a moment ago. She thought about what staying close to Louis was going to cost her and what it was going to cost him, and she said nothing and waited for Goebbels to leave so she could be alone with those thoughts in the dark.

* * *

Germany. The Schmeling Estate.

The dining room of the Schmeling estate was large enough to seat twenty, but they used it for two. Max and Annie Ondra sat at opposite ends of the long table in clothes that were formal enough for an occasion, though there was none.

The china was very good. The wine was better. Annie held her glass and looked at her husband down the length of the table.

"I don't know why you have to go back to America for this fight."

"The Fuhrer has his reasons."

"Why? The Fuhrer should showcase Berlin for the great city that it is."

Max set down his fork. He looked at his wife with the patient, slightly tired expression of a man who has explained something before and is preparing to explain it again.

"You worry too much, my dear. I will defeat Joe Louis again and return a hero once more."

Annie looked at him. She was a beautiful woman known throughout Europe as one of its finest actresses, and she had married a man whose fame had outshone her own. She had learned over the years that famous men have a quality of certainty that is sometimes wisdom and sometimes the inability to imagine that things can go wrong for them.

Max wiped his lips with the linen napkin, pushed back from the table, and rose.

His eyes rolled back.

It was not gradual. There was no warning except the slight stiffening that preceded it by half a second, not long enough for anyone to act on. His hand shot out, found the tablecloth, and gripped it, but it did not help. He went down, pulling the china with him, the plates and glasses and the good silverware all following him to the floor in a loud cascade.

Annie was around the end of the table before the last piece stopped moving. She looked down at her husband, at his eyes fixed and dilated and aimed at the ceiling, at the convulsions moving through his body in waves.

She screamed.

* * *

The hospital room had the hush of a place where machines were doing the work that bodies should be doing for themselves. Tubes ran into Schmeling from several directions at once, delivering fluids into his veins with thinner lines in his nose and into the corners of his mouth. The machines tracking his condition produced their soft, steady sounds, and the man in the bed was barely recognizable as the man who had stood in the center of the Berchtesgaden party and assumed a fighting stance to the delight of the most powerful men in Germany.

What they had made of him had cost. This was one of them.

Josef Mengele stood at the foot of the bed with Schmeling's chart in his hands. He was a trim man with careful eyes and the manner of a physician who has decided that the interesting question is never the patient's comfort but always something else, something further along and more instructive. Medicine as inquiry. The patient as data. His assistant, Dr. Rudolf Fuchs, stood a step behind him with a notepad, which was where Fuchs always stood, at the precise angle of a man who had been trained to record without intruding.

Goebbels came through the door.

"Doctor Mengele, what have you found?"

Mengele looked up from the chart.

"It was as I suspected. There was a massive dehydration of virtually all bodily fluids: lymphatic, pericardial, and cerebrospinal. We are replacing them with the electro-ionized stem cell fluid."

"He must fight again. The Fuhrer himself insists upon it. Do you understand that?"

"Yes. We'll soon see if Mr. Schmeling's body agrees."

Fuchs wrote something on his notepad. The machines continued.

The tubes ran from Schmeling's arms and throat across the floor of the room to a glass tank set against the far wall. Goebbels followed them with his eyes, tracing them the way you trace something when you are not in a hurry to see the end. Inside the tank, several fetuses floated in a purplish, glowing fluid, their navels connected to the tubes. They were of various sizes, the largest near term. A large metallic orb mounted above the tank sent blue electricity dancing across the surface of the fluid in patterns that had no natural analog.

Goebbels looked at the tank for a long moment.

"These are Jew fetuses, no?"

"Of course, Herr Goebbels. We are not going to abort Aryan babies."

"I'm not sure the Fuhrer would approve of Jew fluids regenerating our champion."

Mengele set the chart down. He looked at Goebbels directly,

calculating the consequences the truth might have.

"You know as well as I do that the genetic inferiority argument is a specious one."

The room was very quiet except for the machines and the sound the orb made.

Goebbels was quiet for a moment. Then he said something that he would never say anywhere that could be recorded, in a voice pitched below what Fuchs's pen could reach.

"Of course. The Jews are actually superior to many of our sausage-eating bumpkin 'Aryans.'"

Mengele looked at him. The admission sat in the room between them.

"Their success made them the perfect enemy for the Fuhrer."

Goebbels nodded. He turned toward the far end of the room, to the glass partition. Beyond it, a larger space was dimly lit. He walked toward it.

"How are our next generation of Ubermenschen doing?"

Behind the glass, a massive tank of the same purple fluid occupied the center of the adjacent space. Hundreds of fetuses floated in it, connected by their tubes to a system that pulsed with the slow, deliberate rhythm of something mechanical pretending to be biological. From the tank, more tubes ran to the forearms of five men strapped upright to vertical beds along the back wall. The men were unconscious. Their faces were in shadow. What was not in shadow was their size, which registered before anything else. The sheer scale of what was in those beds, the width of the shoulders and the length of the limbs, all of it pushing past the boundary of what nature intended men to become.

"Beautifully, Reich Minister," Mengele said. "They will be at full strength for the attack."

Goebbels looked at the five silhouettes for a long moment. The blue electricity moved across the surface of the tank. The machines continued their accounting. Fuchs continued to write.

Nobody said anything else. There was nothing else that needed saying.

* * *

Washington, D.C. A Private Office.

Donovan was already standing when Joe came in, which was either courtesy or strategy or both. He extended a hand, and Joe took it. Mercer was there. Hoover was there with Tolson beside him as always, close enough to be a unit.

"Joe, I'm sure you recognize J. Edgar Hoover and his associate, Clyde Tolson."

Joe looked at them.

"G-men."

Mercer cleared his throat.

"The skater you've been seeing, Sonja Henie..."

"What about her?"

"She's a Nazi spy," Hoover said.

Joe looked at Donovan. He trusted Donovan.

"It's true, Joe."

Mercer opened a folder and spread photographs on the desk. The Weegee pictures of Joe and Sonja through the bungalow window at the Beverly Hills Hotel. Joe looked at them with the expression of a man confronting evidence of something he thought had been secret and personal.

"The Nazis were going to use these to destroy you."

"That don't prove Sonja was involved."

"How long did it take you to bed her?" Tolson asked, speaking only after seeing Hoover unable to find his own words.

"That's none of your damn business."

"She slept with you the first night," Hoover said. "One of the biggest movie stars in Hollywood risks her entire career to sleep with a Negro? Even you can understand the folly of that."

Joe looked at Hoover. He took his time over it.

"What the hell you know about what attracts women to men?"

The question landed in the room, and Hoover absorbed it in silence, which was the only option available to him.

"Not a damn thing," Donovan said. "But she's a Nazi spy through and through."

Joe looked at him. Donovan held the look.

"We have agents in Germany. Sonja has visited with both Hitler and Goebbels."

Mercer put another photograph on the desk. This one showed Sonja with Goebbels. She was laughing. Her hands were on him in the easy, familiar way of someone who is comfortable with the person they are touching. Joe looked at it for a long time.

"She's a double-crossing Nazi whore," Hoover said.

Joe's right hand came up before he decided to raise it. Hoover moved behind Tolson with a speed that suggested he had planned this exit in advance.

"You watch your mouth."

"You're not the only American she's *compromising*," Tolson said.

"She travels in exclusive circles," Hoover said, "with very powerful men. Captains of industry."

Joe looked at the photographs again. He looked at the picture of Sonja and Goebbels. He looked at it long enough to arrive somewhere on the other side of the first reaction, which was the place where truth lived, whether you wanted it or not.

"So, watchu want from me?"

"We want you to kill her, Joe."

The room was very quiet.

"What?! No. No way."

"Joe, this is the kind of mission you signed up for."

"Killing a woman? What kind of test is that?"

"It's not a test of your strength," Hoover said, stepping out slightly from behind Tolson. "It's a test of your willingness to do what it takes to win a war, whatever the cost. It's a test of whether your country can count on you."

"My country has always been able to count on me," Joe said. He didn't finish the statement in reverse, however, but Hoover got it just the same.

* * *

Hollywood. A Sound Stage.

The song was called Chattanooga Choo Choo, and it filled the sound stage with the joy that only a great piece of music can. *Is that the Chattanooga Choo Choo?* The cameras were rolling, and the crew was working on the set. Sonja moved across the ice in the lights, and the whole thing had the quality of a dream.

Joe stood in the wings and watched.

She moved the way she always moved, with the economy of someone for whom this was not a performance but simply the natural expression of what she was. She was luminous. Joe watched her. The photograph of her hands on Goebbels sat in his jacket pocket. He wanted to tear it up and throw it away, but he hadn't.

He watched her finish the scene. He listened as the director called "cut." He watched the crew move in around her. He turned and walked away from the wings, back through the corridor between the sound stages, his hat down and his coat collar up.

Behind him, two silhouettes peeled away from the crowd and followed.

Joe expected this. He had been expecting it since the private office meeting with Hoover. He kept walking and did not look back. He turned down the corridor toward the dressing rooms and counted the footsteps that were not his own. He waited for half an hour, barely moving. The men were there, just around the corner, and he knew that they weren't moving either.

Finally, he went to Sonja's dressing room door.

Behind him, the footsteps stopped when his did.

He knocked.

The door opened, and Sonja was there. Her face did the thing it always did, which was to become readable, to become a face that was not managing or hiding anything. She came forward into his arms. She tried to kiss him.

He turned away.

"Joe, what's wrong?"

He said nothing. He looked at her with the photograph still in his jacket pocket and the meeting still in his head and something else underneath both of those things, something that had been building since the Beverly Hills garden when he had danced with her in the dark and told himself that California was different and knew it wasn't true.

He had trusted her.

"Joe, you're scaring me. What is it?"

He grabbed her by the arms, up near her shoulders. She couldn't move against his overwhelming strength.

"Stop. You're hurting me."

"You working for Hitler?"

"What? No..."

His right hand left her arm and went to her throat. Not hard. Not yet. He could feel her pulse against his palm, fast and present, the pulse of a woman who was frightened and not pretending otherwise.

"One more time. Are you?!"

What happened next was something he had not anticipated and would not forget. Instead of fighting it, Sonja took hold of his wrist with both of hers and pressed it harder against her throat. Her face began to change color. The vein at her neck stood out against the pressure. Her eyes were open, and they did not leave his.

She was not fighting him. She was helping him kill her.

He tried to pull his hand back. She held it with a strength he had not expected. He had to force it free, and he did, and she fell back onto the couch and lay there with her hand at her own throat now, finding her breath in stages, the color returning to her face slowly and without drama. When she could speak, she spoke.

"You should have let me die."

Joe stood in the center of the small room, looked at her, and tried to find the version of this moment that made sense.

"I was a Nazi agent... but that was before..."

"Before what?"

"Before I fell in love with you."

"You expect me to believe that?"

"You do believe it because you love me too. I know you do."

She looked up at him. The heartbreak in her face was not feigned. He had seen heartbreak performed in enough places, and he knew that it was her skating that made her a movie star, not her acting, which was only passable.

He sat down on the couch beside her. He put his arms around her. He held her while the sound from the stage came through the walls; the crew wrapping up for the night, voices calling to each other in the ordinary language of people who did not know what was happening in this room.

"They threatened to kill my family," she said. Her voice was steady now, the steadiness of reporting a fact she had had time to consider. "It's not an excuse. Not a good enough one, anyway."

Joe thought about a truck on a road in Alabama. He thought about a noose and a cousin and the weight of a man's collarbone giving way under his fist.

"Maybe it is. My family was threatened once, too."

She pulled back and looked at him.

"What are we going to do?!"

"Right now, we gotta get outta here."

He got up and went to the door, opened it a crack, and looked down the corridor in both directions. The corridor was long, and well lit, and at the far end of it, where it turned back toward the main sound stage, two men stood trying not to look like they were just standing there.

He let the door close.

"Hoover's G-men are out there. They're here to kill you if I can't."

Chapter 8

Hollywood.

One moment, there was a wall. Then, there was a sound of thunder and a hole the size and shape of a large man's fist and forearm driven through plaster with a force that sent debris into the night air.

Then Joe came through the debris, followed by Sonja.

The four G-men who were positioned outside thought they had everything in hand, only to suddenly find out they didn't. Joe looked at them and quickly calculated their running speed, Sonja's running speed, his running speed, and his running speed while carrying Sonja. He scooped Sonja up into his arms and ran.

The G-men moved. They were fast men, trained men, men who had been selected and conditioned for exactly this kind of situation. Joe left them behind in approximately four strides.

Two cars started up and came after him.

Hollywood at night was a city that slowed down but never entirely stopped. The streets had traffic and pedestrians even at this hour. Joe ran through it with Sonja's arms around his neck, her face pressed against his shoulder. She had never moved more quickly, even on skates.

Joe twisted his body as they moved between cars. The headlights of the G-men's cars swept the street behind him. He heard the engines working harder.

Inside the lead car, one of the G-men looked at the speedometer. Fifty miles an hour.

"Holy shit!"

Joe was pulling away from them.

The G-man in the passenger seat produced his revolver and leaned out the window. The first shot cracked through the night air, and Joe heard it. He darted to the left before a second bullet could find the mark.

Sonja felt him moving under her, the weight shifting left and right with a timing that seemed impossible at this speed. She kept her eyes closed and trusted.

Up ahead, an overpass. The road curved under it, and the G-men's cars would follow the road. Joe looked at the overpass and then out into the distance. He jumped.

The leap carried him up and forward in a high arc that cleared twenty feet of vertical space as though gravity weren't a fact, and he landed on the overpass above with Sonja still in his arms. He stood and looked down at the street below, where the two cars were screeching to a halt, the drivers craning their necks upward at something they could not account for.

Joe looked down at them for a moment.

* * *

Los Angeles. Union Station.

The PA announcer had been making announcements in this

building for so long that his words just blended into the background unless you had a need to hear them.

"Last call for the 9:30 to Washington D.C. on platform seven."

Joe and Sonja slipped through the station with their hats down and their collars up, which was their best available disguise and not a very good one. The station was not crowded at this hour, but it was not empty either.

They passed the lounge. Inside, customers sat with their drinks, and a radio played, and nobody looked up.

Then a cop ahead of them did look up.

He was a young cop with a pleasant face, and he recognized Joe. It startled him into a smile.

The radio in the lounge shifted. The music stopped.

"Americans everywhere are urged to be on the lookout for heavyweight boxer Joe Louis and movie star Sonja Henie. If sighted, call police or your local branch of the FBI immediately."

The cop's smile went cold as his face sank. His hand went to his holster.

Joe grabbed Sonja's hand. They ran.

"Freeze, Louis!"

A shot cracked through the station, and the people who had been minding their business stopped minding their business and screamed and scattered.

Joe and Sonja ran into the entrance to the train platform, and then they were on the platform as the train was pulling away. The cop came through the entrance behind them.

He stopped.

He looked left and right and forward and back. The platform was still. No Joe. No Sonja. He turned in a full circle. He looked at the train. It was too far out. They couldn't have boarded it. He scratched his head.

On the roof of the departing train, Joe and Sonja lay flat and still, moving east into the California night.

* * *

The moonlight was generous, and the train's clacking journey through it had a quality that was almost peaceful if you were not lying on the roof of a train and wanted by the FBI. The countryside opened up around them as Hollywood fell behind, revealing the dark shapes of hills and then flatland, and then the beginning of the desert.

Joe put his arm around her. The wind at this speed came at them steady and cold. He pulled her closer. They sat in silhouette against the sky, two people on top of a train going east. The motion and the moonlight and the leisurely quality of being nowhere in particular while moving fast might have looked romantic from a distance, but it was anything but.

"You're freezing."

"I'm all right."

He stood. He offered her his hand.

"What?"

"Let's go inside."

"But..."

"It's late enough. Bound to be somewhere to bed down."

She took his hand. She stood. He moved to the side of the train and went over the edge and down to a door, his hands finding purchase on the metal with the easy certainty of someone for whom the side of a moving train presented no particular challenge. The door was locked from the inside. He worked it briefly, and the lock broke to his will.

He offered his hand back up to Sonja. She took it.

* * *

The black porter's name was Homer, and he had been working this line for eleven years, which was long enough to have seen most of the things a man could see on a cross-country train between Los Angeles and Washington. He had not seen this.

He turned the corner into the narrow corridor and came face-to-face with Joe Louis.

He stood very still. Joe Louis stood very still. Sonja stood behind Joe Louis and also stood very still. For a moment, the three of them occupied the corridor in a silence that had several layers. Homer knew Joe was wanted by the authorities. Joe didn't know what he was going to do about it.

Homer put his finger to his lips. He gestured them toward the back of the train.

The porters' quarters were at the rear. It was a small room designed for six men that six men were currently using, three of them in a card game around a fold-out table and the other three in their bunks. The room smelled of tobacco and hair oil and the body odor of men who worked hard and slept in a small space. It was, Joe thought, not entirely unlike rooms he had grown up in.

When they entered, the card game stopped. The men in the bunks opened their eyes. Six faces registered what they were looking at, and what they were looking at was Joe Louis. Perhaps even more surprising was the appearance of a beautiful white woman whose fame was almost the equal of Joe's.

One of the stunned porters opened his mouth.

Homer's hand came down over it.

"Boys," Homer said, in a voice pitched just above the sound of the train, "we got some guests tonight."

They sat frozen.

"Well, one of you knuckleheads stand up and let this young lady sit down," Homer said.

A porter stood up.

"I don't want to be a bother," Sonja said.

"Miss, please sit," Homer said.

Joe nodded, and Sonja sat, and then the porters were on their feet and moving toward Joe in a wave, hands extended, and for a few minutes the small room was full of the gayest noise imaginable. Handshakes and back-slaps and the low, urgent voices of people who know they should not be loud and cannot entirely help it.

"You didn't do nothing, did ya?"

"They always blame the black man."

Joe let it wash over him and shook every hand and received every slap, some of them twice, and said the things that needed to be said. He felt something in the room that he recognized from other rooms and from gyms and church halls, and from the streets of Black Bottom. It was the warmth of being known by people who cared about you, even if they didn't know you well. It was not the same as what white crowds gave him. White crowds gave him spectacle and recognition. This was acceptance.

As they chatted, Homer left and came back from the dining car with a sandwich wrapped in a napkin. He held it out to Joe.

Joe took it and nodded his thanks, and then gave half of it to Sonja.

They sat for a while with the sound of the surrounding train: the click-clack of it over the joints in the rails, the small shifts and settlings of the car. Sonja fell asleep against the wall with Joe's jacket over her, her breathing slow and even. One of the other porters had his mouth open and was producing a sound that was technically snoring, but so loud that snoring wasn't an adequate name for it. The card table was folded back against the wall. The room had the peace of men who worked hard and slept without difficulty.

Homer looked at his hands on his knees. He was not a man who talked easily. Joe had figured this out within the first five minutes of knowing him and had respected it. The easy talkers were never the ones worth waiting for.

"Sorry about the cramped quarters."

Joe looked around the small room. At the sleeping men. At the fold-out table. At the window, and the desert dark beyond it, and the stars above that.

"Reminds me of home." Joe meant it. Not as a complaint and not as a compliment. Just as a fact. "But, look, I don't want y'all to get in any trouble. We'll jump off next stop."

"Nonsense. You're our guests all the way to D.C. Ain't nobody ever comes back here to this room nohow."

Joe smiled. "Thank you, Homer."

Homer looked at him. He took his time.

"No. Thank you, Mr. Louis."

"For what?"

"For what? Making me feel like a man, instead of the boy I been called all my life. It's all of us in that ring with you when you fight, Joe."

One of the sleeping porters shifted in his bunk and resettled and went on sleeping.

"And you weren't just fighting the Nazis. You were fighting every white person who ever looked down their damned noses at us and made us feel small and pointless. Thank you for that."

He paused. The train moved through the dark.

"You don't even know what you are to the rest of us, do you?"

Joe looked at him uncertainly.

"You're a kind of hero to us. More than that, really. Like a superhero."

The word landed in the room with a weight that comes from being exactly right. Joe felt something move in his chest. His eyes went hot. He smiled, but that was only to keep from crying. Homer saw it, and it got to him, too.

"Hey, come on now, man, you don't want me to see the great Joe Louis bawling like a baby, do you?"

Joe reached out and put his right hand on Homer's shoulder, and pulled him in, and held him. Homer smiled with his eyes wet, and neither of them said anything for a bit as the train moved east through the American dark.

Joe pulled back. He looked at Homer.

"Superhero, you said?"

"I did."

"Mind if I use that?"

Chapter 9

Eastern United States.

The landscape outside the train windows had been changing for hours: the desert giving way to the scrubland of the Southwest, then the red earth of the middle states, then the gradual greening of the east as the train worked its way toward the Atlantic.

Joe sat and watched it all pass.

* * *

Washington, D.C. The White House.

The fence was wrought iron, and it was not, Joe had to admit, much of a fence.

"You'd think the White House would be better protected," Joe said.

"Yeah," Sonja said.

The grounds beyond it were dark, and the residence beyond the grounds was lit, and somewhere inside it, the meeting they needed to be at was happening without them.

"Still, it's best you wait here."

Sonja looked at him.

"We're in this together. So, we're going to see the president. Together." She paused. "Besides, I hear he likes my movies."

Joe looked at her. She was in the same clothes she had been wearing on the sound stage, her hair loose now, her eyes very clear in the light from the street. He had been thinking about this woman and what she was and what she might be for most of the past several hours, and he had not arrived at any conclusion that simplified things.

Joe positioned himself by the fence. Sonja backed away several steps. She looked at Joe. She took a running start right at him and leaped, and he caught her and launched her up and over the fence in one motion, and she went over in a clean arc and landed on the other side the way she landed on ice, which was to say exactly right.

Joe turned to the fence and went over it in a hop and a sideways swing of his legs.

They ran across the grounds toward the residence.

Two Secret Service agents on patrol turned at the sound of footsteps, saw them, and started after them. Joe and Sonja kept moving, angling toward the rear of the building. A window showed light, and an agent inside looked out and saw them.

Sonja glanced behind her at the two agents closing the distance.

"Joe!"

Joe looked up. The second floor. That was the only way.

"Jump on!"

She got on his back, her arms around his neck, her legs around his waist, and he went up the side of the building with his hands finding purchase on the stonework, moving fast enough that the agents below were still processing what they were watching when he reached the balcony above. Joe got a leg over the balcony railing, and then he was on it, and Sonja was off his back. He reared back and put his foot through the balcony door.

Two Secret Service agents were inside. Guns up.

"Freeze!"

* * *

The White House. Situation Room.

The meeting had the low-grade tension of a room full of men who disagreed about something important. Roosevelt was at the head of the table. Donovan was standing at a board covered in photographs of tanks massed along a border. Hoover was with Tolson. The Joint Chiefs were arranged along the walls.

Donovan was making his case.

"Mr. President, these are photographs from our agents on the ground in Germany. These are Von Rundstadt's 8th, 10th, and 14th armies moving toward the Polish border. If they attack, England and France will have no alternative but to declare war."

Roosevelt looked at the map. He had the look of a man who had been carrying a burden that would not be easily put down.

"Bill, there's no good way for me to say this, but we're folding OSS under the FBI's authority."

Donovan looked at him.

"What?!"

"You'll keep your job, but you'll report directly to J. Edgar."

"Frank, you can't do this to me. I'll resign before I report to this... ferret!"

"Goddamn it, Bill, this isn't about you, it's about the country!"

"This is because of Joe Louis, isn't it?"

"I trusted you, and you made the wrong call."

The door to the Situation Room came off its hinges.

Not metaphorically. The two Secret Service agents from the balcony came through it at speed, leaving full body silhouettes in the shattered wood, and then they were on the floor, and Joe was in the doorway with Sonja behind him, and for a brief moment, the room stopped because grown men being hurled through the door was not on the agenda.

Donovan's gun came up. It was aimed at Joe's head.

"Shoot him!" Hoover said.

Roosevelt looked at Joe. Joe looked at Roosevelt.

"More agents are coming, Joe," Roosevelt said. "You can't defeat them all."

"I trust Mr. Donovan, and I trust you, Mr. President. Please let me say my piece. You don't like what I have to say, you can arrest me and Sonja."

Roosevelt nodded.

"By the authority vested in me, I arrest you right now!"

Donovan lowered the gun.

"Aw, dry up, Hoover."

Roosevelt looked at Joe for a long moment. The room waited.

"All right, Joe, the floor is yours."

"I'm no traitor, sir. And Sonja was forced to work for Hitler 'cause he threatened to kill her family. But she's gonna make up for that. She's got a plan. Sonja..."

Sonja stepped forward.

"I will return to Germany and spy for you."

Donovan looked at her. The look was not warm.

"Back to the laps of your Nazi cohorts."

"You saying she should have let them kill her family?" Joe asked.

Hoover found his position. "Tough times require a level of courage you would know nothing about, Mr. Louis."

Joe moved toward him. Sonja's hand came out and stopped him.

"He's right, Joe. I should have made that choice."

The room was quiet. This was not what anyone had expected her to say, and the unexpectedness of it landed and changed the temperature.

"The war that's coming is bigger than anyone's family, mine included. Hitler must be stopped. No sacrifice is too great. I know that now."

Roosevelt watched them. He watched the way Joe looked at her and the way she looked at him, and he said nothing.

Sonja turned to Roosevelt.

"Mr. President, Hitler and Goebbels trust me. I can get information that no one else can. I can help you save thousands of lives."

"She's telling the truth," Joe said.

Roosevelt looked at him.

"How do you know?"

"Because I been lied to my whole life. I got pretty damn good at knowing when somebody's telling the truth."

"Oh, for god's sake!" Hoover said.

"Mr. Donovan's never lied to me. Not once," Joe said.

Donovan shot a look Joe's way. Then he turned to Roosevelt.

"Mr. President, sending her back is our best chance to figure out exactly what the Germans are up to. I know they're planning something big."

"Who would trust her?" Hoover shouted.

Donovan moved to another photograph on the board. The Port of Hamburg. Warships in various stages of construction. And one structure that stood apart from the others was a covered dock, enormous, its contents invisible from any angle the camera had been able to achieve.

"This is a top-secret dock in Hamburg," Donovan said. "We haven't been able to get agents inside, so we don't know what they're building. We do know it's vital that we find out. Sonja might be able to do that."

Roosevelt looked at the photograph, then at Joe. He was a man who had made a great many decisions that other people had to live with, and he had made them with the available information, which was seldom complete. But life and death choices had to be made, anyway.

"Well, Bill, Joe, and Miss Henie just bought you a second chance."

"What?!" Hoover's voice climbed. "You can't be serious! You're not sending her back to her friends, are you?"

"I am!"

The room went quiet. Hoover subsided. Roosevelt turned to Donovan.

"Bill, how do we get Miss Henie back to Germany so it doesn't look like she's cooperating with us?"

"They know we're looking for her. Let them think she was the clever spy who got away."

"Mr. President, I should go with her," Joe said.

Roosevelt shook his head. Not harshly. He had already thought about this and arrived at the answer.

"Joe, you've got the biggest fight of your life coming up in New York. You have to lick Max Schmeling and win back the title for your country."

"But that's just a boxing match-"

"No, it's much more than that, Joe. It's our best against their best. When you beat Schmeling, the American people will know that they can beat Germany."

Joe said nothing. He looked at the photographs on the board: the tanks, the border, the covered dock in Hamburg that hid something nobody yet knew the shape of. He thought about Donovan's lab under the Washington Mall and the footage of himself at the bottom of a swimming pool and Homer's face in the porters' quarters when the tears nearly came. He thought about a word.

The word was *superhero*. Homer had said it first. Joe thought it odd the way the right words always get said by the person who gave them away. Joe turned the meaning of the word over in his mind. It had nothing to do with tights or a shield, and it wasn't something cooked up in a secret basement lab in Washington. It was the story of a man who stands up when standing up costs something. A man who fights the battles that must be fought, even if they never make the history books. A man who carries other people's hopes because he happens to be strong enough to hold them without breaking.

That was something he could do.

Sonja put her hand on his.

"He's right, Joe. And what I have to do, I can only do by myself."

She looked up at him.

"You must defeat Max Schmeling. Your country is counting on it."

"Your country is counting on you, too," Joe said. "They just may not know it yet."

Chapter 10

New York Harbor.

The fog had come in off the water and made itself at home in the space between the dock lights and the dark water below. The foghorn sounded its long, mournful note across the harbor, and it echoed back, softened and more pleasant.

Joe and Sonja stood concealed near the gangplank of a German cargo ship. Around them, the dock was busy with the noise and activity of a vessel preparing to sail: the creak of lines under tension, the clatter of cargo being secured, voices calling orders to each other in German.

Joe looked at her in the fog light and thought about the Beverly Hills garden and their train journey with its small dressing room, the porters' quarters, and Homer's word and all the distance between the beginning of this adventure, this love story, this mission, this awakening. He couldn't say exactly what it was in simple terms. He had not planned any of it.

"You come back to me safe and sound, you hear?"

"I will, Joe, I promise."

The fog made halos around the dock lights, and her face was in the soft center of one of them.

"All of a sudden I feel real small, in a big ol' world spinning out of control."

Sonja put her hand over his heart.

"As long as we have each other, the rest of the world doesn't matter."

She kissed him. It was not a brief kiss. It was deep, and it carried everything that had been said and everything that hadn't. When she pulled back, her eyes were bright, and she did not try to hide it.

"Goodbye, my love."

The emotion overcame her, and she turned and walked quickly up the gangplank. Joe watched her go. He watched until she disappeared into the ship and the fog had closed around the place where she had been, and there was nothing left to watch.

He stood there for another moment, anyway.

* * *

Pompton Lakes, New Jersey. Training Camp.

The poster on the wall said FIGHT OF THE CENTURY. JOE LOUIS VS. MAX SCHMELING. YANKEE STADIUM. Someone had drawn a fist around the words in red ink and taped it to the post at the corner of the ring, which was where Joe could see it every time he worked the near corner.

He was working the near corner now. The sparring partner across from him was a large man and a game one, and he had been willing to take the punishment that came with the job of standing in for Schmeling, but that willingness had limits, and those limits were becoming apparent.

Joe settled into his stance and threw a body shot. The sparring partner's feet left the canvas.

Roxborough climbed through the ropes.

"Joe, go easy. We're running out of sparring partners."

"Sorry," Joe said, turning to the sparring partner. "You okay?"

The sparring partner looked at him from behind the padded mask that covered most of his face.

"Not really."

A cluster of reporters pressed against the rope at ringside, notebooks out, pencils moving. One voice found the gap between the sparring partner's answer and whatever came next.

"Joe, since Schmeling knocked you out last time, are you scared?"

Joe looked at the reporter. He let the question sit for a moment.

"Hell yes, I'm scared. I'm scared I might kill him."

The reporters laughed. Roxborough put a hand on Joe's shoulder and steered him toward the ring steps. He knew exactly how much pressure to apply.

A second reporter got a question in before they reached the steps.

"Do you see this fight as Joe Louis versus Max Schmeling, or America against Germany?"

Joe stopped. He thought about what Donovan had said in the Situation Room, and what Roosevelt had said, and what Homer had said in the dark of the porters' quarters, and what the word *superhero* meant when you unpacked it all the way down to its foundation.

"It's just me against him."

He saw the disappointment in their eyes. The reporters

wanted something larger, and they were not wrong to want it, because this was something larger.

"But, yeah, in another way, it's bigger than that. Us against them. Freedom against fascism, I guess you could say."

He and Roxborough moved off toward the locker room. Joe kept his voice low.

"If we actually had freedom here," Joe whispered to Roxborough.

Roxborough said nothing. It was the right response and also the only honest one.

* * *

Port of Hamburg.

The cargo ship docked in the early light with the morning fog on the water, the gulls making their noise above the harbor, and Goebbels waiting at the foot of the gangplank with an SS detachment behind him.

"Sonja!"

He threw his arms around her and administered the European double-cheek kiss.

"So good to see you, Josef!"

"I was so relieved when I got your radio message. I was sure the Americans had captured you."

"They nearly did. I was able to convince the Schwartze that I loved him, and he smuggled me aboard the ship."

Goebbels looked at her with the expression of a man encountering information that does not quite compute.

"He believed something so ridiculous?"

Sonja was not an actress first and foremost, but Hollywood had taught her a few things, and her acting was steadily improving. For this, she could have won an Oscar.

"Negroes are easy to fool."

Goebbels beamed. He took her arm, and they walked up the dock with the SS detachment falling in behind them, and Sonja looked at the harbor and the city behind it and thought about Joe standing alone in the fog.

* * *

Hamburg. Goebbels' Private Office.

The ceiling of Goebbels' private office was ornate because powerful men seemed to need to make things ornate. It wasn't because beauty was the goal, but because expense was the signal of power, and expense had been applied liberally to every surface. Sonja looked at the ceiling. She had become an expert at looking at ceilings.

Goebbels rolled off her with the satisfaction of a man who has no capacity to understand the difference between what is given and what is endured. He reached for his gold cigarette case on the nightstand, extracted a cigarette, and lit it.

"Oh, how I've dreamed of that, my dear."

"As have I, Josef. Your sexual prowess is something to behold." She wanted to add the words *from a great distance,* but she knew better.

"You bring out the animal in me, Schotzie."

He smiled and drew on the cigarette, and looked very pleased with himself. Sonja sat up and reached for the sheet. As she did, she saw something that sent a cold charge through her entire body.

Hitler was standing in the doorway, watching them.

Goebbels scrambled.

"Fuhrer!"

He gave the salute from the bed, which was one of the more undignified things Sonja had witnessed, and there had been competition for that title. Sonja pulled the sheet up, and met Hitler's eyes, and held them the way she had learned to hold them.

"Hello, Sonja, welcome home."

"Thank you, my Fuhrer."

"We are needed at the port, Reich Minister."

As Goebbels jumped out of bed with the obedient speed of a lapdog, Sonja's hand moved quietly to the nightstand and closed around the gold cigarette case, which was monogrammed with his initials, JG. She held it under the sheet.

* * *

Washington, D.C., Hoover's Apartment.

The study was the room of a man who maintained careful appearances and kept his real business elsewhere. Hoover moved through it with the quick, certain step of a man going somewhere he had been many times, and he went to the bookshelf and pressed something behind the third volume from the left on the second shelf. A panel opened in the wall.

He went through it. He closed it behind him.

The room inside was small and functional, and contained a

telegraph machine and a set of headphones. Hoover sat down, put on the headphones, and began tapping.

The message went to Berlin. Berlin sent it to Hamburg. In Hamburg, a telegraph operator deciphered it, went pale, and reached for his phone.

"Get me the Gestapo."

* * *

Port of Hamburg.

Hitler and Goebbels moved quickly down a semi-hidden hallway and then down a long, narrow flight of stairs, their footsteps swallowed by the stone around them. The SS detachment followed. They reached a door at the bottom and went through it.

The covered dock on the other side of the door was large enough to contain a small city. The smell of it hit first. Hot metal and machine oil, and the electric bite of arc welders, and the river smell of the harbor coming through the gaps in the enormous roof. The noise came second. Hydraulic rivet guns and the deep bass thrum of machinery, and beneath all of it, the sound of something very large being prepared for a dangerous purpose.

Sonja had come down the stairs thirty seconds behind them. She had been stopped on the dock by two SS men. She bluffed her way through by showing them Goebbels's monogrammed gold cigarette case and informing them how furious he would be not to have it. The men knew about his affair with Henie because Goebbels had made sure everyone knew about the affair, with the exception of his wife. He was too much the narcissist to keep such a conquest a secret.

Sonja was inside now, in the shadows of the upper level, moving along the catwalk toward the rafters, her hands finding the metal above her with the sureness of someone who was so athletic she had found international fame because of it.

She located her position and looked down.

The U-boat below her was the largest thing she had ever seen inside a building. It dominated the covered dock the way a field dominates a stadium. It was the thing around which everything else had organized itself. Workers swarmed over it with the focused urgency of men working against a life-or-death deadline. The front end of the submarine stood open like a hatch, and into it, slowly and with great mechanical care, an enormous weapon was being loaded. It was the size of a building. It had the shape of a torpedo scaled up by someone who had lost all sense of proportion, or by someone who had loaded so much TNT into one place it needed a container larger than any that had ever been built.

Hitler walked to a podium at the far end of the dock. A massive screen behind him came alive with his image, projected large enough to be visible from every corner of the space. The crew of the U-boat rose as one, along with hundreds of soldiers and sailors filling the dock floor.

"Heil Hitler!"

Hitler gave a return salute and held it. The audience waited until he finally lowered it before they sat down. Goebbels sat beside Karl Donitz, the senior commander of the German Navy. Sonja looked at Goebbels from the rafters high above them and kept herself very still.

"Gentlemen, tomorrow this great German vessel sails for New

York City, where we will make a preemptive strike so powerful that we will win the war before it even starts."

In the rafters, Sonja's focus was drawn to the massive submarine. She had seen U-boats before, but this one seemed more than a dozen times larger than any of them.

"The weapon you see being loaded into the U-boat is the single most powerful bomb in the history of the world."

A motion picture replaced Hitler's image on the screen. A village on a hillside, people visible, moving about in the ordinary business of their lives — a woman hanging washing, two children in the street, a man at a cart. Then a bomb struck the hill above the village, and the village ceased to exist. Not destroyed. Vaporized. The hill above it, too. The concussion of it was visible in the way the image shook, because the camera recording it shook from the concussion.

Sonja clung to the rafters and felt the cold of her wet clothes against her skin as she watched the screen and said nothing but felt everything.

"That is a Jew village in Lithuania." He paused. "Or should I say, *was* a Jew village."

The sailors and soldiers rose to their feet, and the sound they made filled the covered dock and echoed off the hull of the U-boat and came back to Sonja in the rafters as something terrifying.

"One week from today, our great champion, Max Schmeling, will fight the black beast, Joe Louis. Our enemies will use the excitement of the bout to distract public attention from their evil actions."

A map of New York City appeared on the screen. The image moved toward the harbor.

"In a secret room aboard the Queen Mary, a group of criminals will be plotting the demise of our Reich. Roosevelt, de Gaulle, Stalin, and Churchill, along with the American Joint Chiefs of Staff, will be among the conspirators. But we will kill them all, along with thousands of New York citizens, to strike a blow from which our foes will never recover."

The men at the dock roared.

Sonja memorized everything. The dimensions of the weapon. The name Donitz. The departure time. The Queen Mary. She laid it down in her memory in order, one fact after another.

Then the Gestapo officers came in. They went to Hitler. Sonja watched them speak. She watched Hitler's face change. The words that changed it floated to her all the way in the rafters.

"Mein Fuhrer, we have just received an urgent message from our American agent, Terrier. Sonja Henie is a double agent, spying for the Americans."

Goebbels rose. Even from the rafters, Sonja could see the shock on his face.

"That can't be! It must be a mistake."

"Terrier is never mistaken," Hitler said.

Hitler glared at him and then looked up, a slow, deliberate movement, scanning the upper reaches of the dock.

"Find Sonja Henie immediately."

Sonja did not wait. She was already moving along the rafter toward the edge of the dock roof. Below her, through a gap, she could see the harbor, the water, the dock, the soldiers already spreading out. There were SS soldiers everywhere she looked.

Behind her, footsteps sounded on the stairs.

She was at the end of the rafter, and also at the end of the line. There were 100 feet of air between her and the water below.

She dove.

It was a clean dive; the product of a body trained for exactly this kind of movement in a different context. Her control was brilliant. She entered the water without a sound and barely a splash. No soul noticed.

She surfaced with only her eyes above the waterline and looked at the dock. Soldiers searching.

She went back underwater.

She came up inside the dock near the front of the U-boat, pulling herself out of the water in the shadow of the enormous hull. The torpedo had been loaded. They were closing the front end. She moved fast and got herself through the gap just as it closed behind her.

The inside of the U-boat was dark and smelled of metal. She stood for a moment, and let her eyes adjust to the darkness, and listened to the surrounding vessel: the hum of its machinery, the voices of sailors somewhere aft. She was in the thick of it now.

* * *

Two days later.

When Sonja moved, she did so carefully, and at night, when most of the sailors were sleeping. She kept to the darkest of the shadows, learning the layout by feel and by sound. The sailors' voices guided her. She used them to know where not to go, threading through the spaces between them.

She heard other sounds when she had worked her way aft. It was lower than the machinery, more deliberate. She followed it.

A hatch door stood slightly open. She looked through the gap.

Dr. Fuchs stood in the room beyond, moving between five cryogenic chambers with his clipboard and his fountain pen, making small adjustments to the dials that controlled the flow of the purple fluid, recording the readings in the careful script of a man for whom the numbers are the point and everything else is secondary. The fluid moved from a large vat through tubes into each of the chambers with a slow, determined rhythm.

Fuchs finished his circuit. He turned toward the door. Sonja flattened herself into the adjacent alcove, and he walked past her without turning his head, his footsteps receding down the corridor.

She slipped into the room.

She moved into the chambers and looked at what was in them and understood for the first time what the Nazis had been building.

The five men were enormous. That was the first thing and the thing that organized everything else around it. Their features had a similarity beneath their individual differences — the white-blonde hair, the massive sloping brows, the outsized mandibles, the bodies that had been built past any natural limit. They lay still in their fluid, not quite alive and not quite dead, waiting for the current to be switched back on.

She thought about what Joe was about to face.

She went to the vat. She found the first switch and flipped it. The fluid stopped flowing into the first chamber.

As she reached for the second switch, the eyes in the first chamber snapped open. They were blue in the way that very few things are blue. The man looked at nothing and everything simultaneously with those eyes, orienting, processing, coming back from wherever the fluid had been keeping him.

Then he opened his mouth, and the scream that came out

filled the room and the corridor beyond it and every adjacent space the submarine contained.

Sonja grabbed Fuchs's fountain pen from the edge of the vat and ran.

She did not get far. A soldier was in the corridor, moving faster than she had expected, and he had her arm before she had fully registered that he was there. She reacted without thought, the fountain pen going into his eye with complete commitment.

The man went to his knees. Blood ran through his fingers as he pitched forward.

Sonja ran down the darkened corridor with the screaming behind her echoing off the metal walls, and the U-boat moving beneath her feet, already turning its enormous hull toward New York City.

Chapter 11

Aboard the U-boat.

The corridor was dark and narrow. Sonja moved through it the way she had been moving through everything for the past several days — without hesitation, without noise, with complete commitment. That was only partly due to personal bravery. She had also run out of options and had to make the most of what remained.

She found the firehose box by feel in the dark, the hatch cover swinging open at her touch. She pulled the hose out and let it trail behind her, down the corridor, around the turn into the narrower passage. Then she waited.

The sailor who came looking found the hose and followed it, which was what she was counting on. He drew his Luger and continued carefully.

Sonja came out of the darkness and brought the heavy brass nozzle of the hose across the side of his head with everything she had. He went down and did not move. She removed his jacket. She took his Luger. She pressed on.

The second hatch was deeper in the boat, down a ladder and through another dark passage. Two sailors were in the room below it, sitting with their cigarettes and their quiet conversation, neither of them expecting what came through the door behind them.

Sonja wrapped the sailor's jacket around her hand, the Luger inside it, and pressed it to the back of the first sailor's head. The shot was muffled by the jacket, so no one outside the room heard it. She'd seen this done in a Cagney movie but was surprised that it worked. The man slumped. The second sailor turned and found the Luger pointed between his eyes and the woman holding it looking at him with an expression that left no room for negotiation. She pulled the trigger. She didn't want to do it, but she had chosen sides, and she was a soldier now. She couldn't play nice and hit him over the head and hope he'd remain unconscious long enough for her to get away. The heroes in movies often did that, not because it made a lick of sense, but because the studio bosses were afraid their stars would lose sympathy. In reality, the stakes were too high. She had to match their cruelty. She had to get her message through no matter the cost.

She emerged from the second hatch onto the deck of the U-boat into the cold night air. The harbor was around her. The lights of New York were in the distance, the water black beneath the stars. Down the deck, Fuchs was conducting a final inspection of the five supermen, who were now very much alive, lined up in their long black trench coats and fedora hats, standing at attention. They had been built for this moment and were ready for it.

Fuchs turned to the captain. "They are ready."

Behind them, thirty feet down the deck, Sonja secretly watched it unfold.

Fuchs raised his arm to the supermen.

"Heil Hitler!"

Five arms went up as one.

"Heil Hitler!"

The inflatable boat was moored to the side of the submarine. The supermen climbed down the ladder one by one and settled into it. One of them unmoored the rope. Another started the engine.

Sonja reached the rail. Below her, the inflatable boat was already moving, the supermen facing forward toward the glittering skyline in the distance. She went over the side, slipped into the water, came up at the stern of the boat, and reached in and found the rope.

The boat motored toward New York.

Sonja held on.

* * *

Yankee Stadium. Dressing Room.

You could hear the crowd even down here. The preliminary bouts were going on, and the noise of the crowd came through the walls, and the floor, and the ceiling like something atmospheric. The echo of it shook things on the shelves.

Chappie worked in silence, which was how Chappie always worked when it mattered. He put Joe's gloves on with the careful deliberateness of a man performing a ritual. He tied them. He taped them. He stepped back and looked at his work.

Mercer came through the door.

Joe looked at him.

"Anything from Sonja?"

"She went radio silent a week ago." Mercer paused. He was

not a man who softened things, which Joe had come to respect about him. "She lied to us, Joe."

"No," Joe said it once and said it flat. "She didn't. She couldn't."

"Then the Nazis caught her. Either way, it's not good."

Joe looked at him. He looked at the space between what Mercer had just said and what it meant if it was true.

"I'm sorry, Joe."

Roxborough came through the door.

"It's time."

Joe looked at Mercer for a moment longer. Then he nodded. He brought his gloves together with a sound that the small room held for a second after the impact, and then he walked out.

* * *

Yankee Stadium. The Ring.

Joe brought his gloves together again in the center of the ring, the same motion, and looked across at Max Schmeling.

The stadium was full. Joe knew it would be, but seeing it still surprised and humbled him. It wasn't just the seats and the faces. It was the quality of attention that seventy thousand people generate when they are all pointed at the same thing. It was electric. Jimmy Stewart was at ringside. Douglas Fairbanks. James Cagney. Bill Donovan sat next to Roosevelt. Hoover and Tolson shared a bag of popcorn and said nothing to each other.

Schmeling across the ring was machine-like in his composure. There was nothing in Schmeling's face that suggested anything needed managing. He had been here before. He had won here before. He believed he would win again, and the belief was so complete it had stopped being belief and become something more like fact.

Joe looked at him.

"I'm gonna kill that Nazi S.O.B.!"

Chappie looked at Joe and smiled. He had heard fighters say things like this many times, but in this instance, he knew it was true.

"I mean it. I'm gonna kill him dead!"

The bell rang.

The two fighters came to the center of the ring.

No feeling out in this one. No early-round caution, no testing, no patience. Joe had his number from the first exchange. The jab went out and found its target. The combinations followed it, and Schmeling was moving backward almost immediately, which was something Schmeling did not do.

The crowd was on its feet.

Joe suddenly threw one of the most vicious body shots in the history of boxing. The sound of it was audible on the upper deck. Schmeling let out a sound that seemed to come from somewhere deeper than the body, a groan that was also an acknowledgment.

Joe continued to attack relentlessly. Not angry exactly, not cruel, but absolutely without mercy. He threw and connected and threw again, and the combinations came in sequences that Chappie had drilled into him over the years in the gym. He was not holding back the way he did with every other fighter he had ever faced. He was not content to hit Schmeling on the shoulder. He was trying to take his head off with every blow.

Schmeling absorbed them and absorbed them, and then a thundering left hook arrived, and Schmeling could not absorb that one.

He went down.

The referee counted. The entire fight lasted only two minutes and four seconds.

The crowd came apart. Joe raised his fists. The referee held up his right hand. Joe looked at the crowd and found his family there — his mother, his father, his sisters, and brothers. Then he found Roosevelt, who was applauding with the unguarded enthusiasm of a man who had set aside being president for a moment in favor of being a human being, and a fight fan who was watching something extraordinary.

Donovan was going crazy beside him.

Hoover threw down his popcorn bag. He and Tolson left.

Joe looked behind him for Schmeling. He wondered if he had gotten up yet or if he was unconscious, but he found the ring empty. He looked toward the doorway and saw the hooded figure walking away with his handlers, head down, moving through the crowd that parted around him, and shouted what crowds often did at the fights.

"Go back to Germany, ya Nazi bum!"

"Say heil to Hitler for me!"

Joe watched him go. Then his mother was in the ring, and her arms were around him, and she was not a small woman. She held him with real force and joy.

"My baby is the heavyweight champ again. I always knew you would change the world!"

Joe held his mother in the ring at Yankee Stadium while seventy thousand people screamed his name all around them. He thought about a great many things, and foremost among them was a Norwegian woman who had gone radio silent a week ago, and whose silence he was not ready to accept as a conclusion.

Donovan looked up at Joe and held his thumb in the air when their eyes met. Roosevelt was in the middle of a group that was leaving the arena, and Donovan quickly caught up to them and left.

Chapter 12

New York Harbor.

The supermen arrived in the inflatable boat as the heavyweight championship fight was ending. They stepped onto the dock one by one with unhurried certainty. They were built for a purpose and were arriving at it. They wore long black trench coats and fedora hats and moved through the dock workers gathered around a radio listening to the fight.

They were seen, but nobody cared. The world wasn't at war. At least not in the minds of the American people.

The leader of the Nazi supermen signaled to one of their spies who was watching from an alcove. A simple nod of the head meant the next part of the plan was on. It was a part that was carried out easily. The spy made a phone call and said, "Go," and two of his colleagues threw a switch that detonated an explosive. It wasn't a large explosive. No one would have viewed it as a prelude to war. More likely, it would have been seen as an accident, a car leaving the road and hitting a power transformer, or a rat biting through a couple of the wrong wires, creating a small explosion as a side effect. What it accomplished, however, was of great importance.

It cut off all phone communication to the dock area of the city.

The attack was on, and the only person who knew it, other than the attackers, was Sonja Henie.

Nobody saw her as she emerged from the water 30 seconds after the supermen started away. She pulled herself onto the dock with the last bit of energy she had, soaking wet and numb from the cold water. Her hands were cramped from clinging to a line for so long.

She looked at the city. She looked at the Queen Mary lit up in the harbor like something from another world. She looked at the supermen moving away from her into the night.

There was no time to rest and recover. She was a world-class athlete, and she knew what it meant to push through pain and exhaustion. The body had a reserve that most people didn't have the will to find. She forced herself to continue.

The fight broadcast was everywhere, coming from radios in windows, from open bars, from the gathering of dock workers thirty feet ahead of her who were on their feet and shouting as the announcer described what was happening at Yankee Stadium. Sonja moved past them without stopping. She loved Joe and was thrilled that he won, but she had something more urgent than a boxing match to attend to.

She saw a phone booth.

She ran to it. She picked up the receiver. She went to dial and stopped. The call cost a nickel, and she had nothing. She looked at the supermen disappearing into the city.

"Dritt!"

Norwegian, but the sentiment was universal.

A man walked past. She turned to him. "Excuse me..."

He looked at her — soaking wet, half a sailor's uniform, something in her eyes that he registered without quite understanding.

"Would you have a nickel?"

He looked at her more carefully. He smiled the smile of a man who thinks he understands a situation.

"Sure, baby. For a kiss."

Sonja reached into the waistband of the sailor's trousers and produced the Luger. The man's smile underwent a rapid transformation. His hand went immediately to his pocket, and he produced all his change and held it out to her, and then he ran.

Sonja picked out a nickel. She inserted it. She dialed.

"I need to speak to Bill Donovan, please. It's urgent!"

The secretary on the other end of the line was not prepared for this moment.

"Mr. Donovan is at the fight."

"Then get me Mercer."

"But, he's listening to the fight..."

"This is Sonja Henie."

A pause.

"The movie star?"

"America is under attack!"

The secretary's smile was almost audible.

"Who is this? Mabel? Nice try, girl!"

"You listen to me. If you want to have a job tomorrow, you tell Mercer, or Donovan, whichever one you can find first, that there is an attack on the Queen Mary and it's underway now!"

"Who told you about the Queen Mary?" the secretary asked, suddenly alert. No one was supposed to know about the meeting on that ship.

"The goddamn Nazis told me! That's who!"

The secretary dropped the phone and sprinted out of the office.

Sonja did much the same. She slammed the phone down, looked up, and saw the Queen Mary docked off in the distance, lit from stem to stern, enormous and oblivious to the danger that approached.

She started running.

* * *

The Queen Mary. Conference Room. Night.

The conference room occupied a large space on one of the upper decks. Churchill had the floor. Roosevelt in his wheelchair, Stalin, DeGaulle, the Joint Chiefs, and military brass from three countries listened intently. Bill Donovan was on the outer ring of the room, near the door, nervously hoping these men would grasp the urgency of the situation, as Churchill had, and believe it.

"Gentlemen, we are at a dire point, I daresay the direst point in the history of civilization," Churchill began.

Stalin leaned forward.

"Why isn't Prime Minister Chamberlain here?"

DeGaulle nodded.

"Yes, I was going to ask the same thing."

Churchill did not miss a beat.

"Mr. Chamberlain is not here, because he is ready to hand 'Herr Schickelgruber'..." He paused to let Hitler's ancestral name sit in the room for a moment, stripped of its theatrical replacement. "...the keys to the hen house."

"What means this hen house?" Stalin asked.

"It means, he will appease Hitler with Poland and Czechoslovakia. It's just a matter of time. Time, we do not have. And then, this wicked little man will attack the rest of Europe. Starting with France, Monsieur DeGaulle."

"This would mean world war, only 20 years after the last one. He would never risk such a thing..."

"That's exactly what he wants you to think," Churchill said.

"Hear, hear," Roosevelt shouted. "Our intelligence officials tell us war is at hand!"

* * *

Inside Joe's dressing room at Yankee Stadium, there was a celebration underway. Chappie, Roxborough, and most of Joe's family were bouncing on their toes, sipping champagne, and hugging each other. It was so raucous that most of them didn't even know that Joe was missing. He was off by himself, sitting on his bench, his mind consumed with things that didn't make sense, or were otherwise unanswered. *Why did Schmeling disappear so quickly? Was Sonja alive? Where had Roosevelt and Donovan gone? Why hadn't they left him instructions? Had all of the cloak and dagger of the last weeks amounted to nothing, and he could simply go back to his old life?*

The answer came quickly when Mercer entered the locker room and found Joe.

"We just heard from Sonja. There's an attack on the Queen Mary underway right now."

"Where's Donovan?"

"The Queen Mary. Everyone's on the Queen Mary. The Germans have cut off communication to the area. I've sent a team down there, but with all the celebration and everyone out on the street…"

Mercer didn't have to finish. Joe was already in a full sprint out of the arena.

* * *

New York. The Streets.

The city was alive with wild celebration of Joe's victory. People were in the streets, drinking openly. Traffic was stalled everywhere, and nothing was moving except the subways.

Above the street, moving at a speed that no ordinary human had ever run, was Joe Louis, wearing his boxing trunks and white robe. He had come out of the stadium and into the night before anyone had fully processed that he was leaving, and now he was racing through New York so quickly that no one who saw him could process it either.

Below his feet, the subway. In front of him, the harbor.

His white robe glowed in the moonlight as he ran. From above, he might have looked like something other than a man. He might have looked like the word Homer had used in the dark of the porters' quarters. A *superhero.*

* * *

New York Harbor.

Joe arrived at the harbor and saw the Queen Mary docked before him, lit and enormous, and started toward it.

Five figures stepped out of the shadows and surrounded him.

They were wearing long black trench coats and fedora hats, and they were extremely large. Joe was usually the biggest man in any room he had entered, but these five made him recalibrate.

As he did, they started moving toward him.

Joe thought fast. "Heil Hitler!" he shouted.

He raised his arm in the salute. All five of them raised their arms automatically in return, which was what training did. It made certain responses involuntary, and in the half-second that their arms were up and their attention was on the salute, Joe grabbed the nearest one's arm at the wrist and yanked it behind him with a single violent motion.

The sound the shoulder made was not a good sound.

The man screamed. Another of them threw a punch at Joe, and Joe moved the screaming man into its path, and the punch landed on him instead, and all the bones in his face broke, and he went down. Joe ran.

They came after him.

He made it to one of the great iron mooring studs set into the dock, still attached to the mooring line that held the Queen Mary in place. He ripped it from the deck — the metal groaning, the bolts giving way, the stud coming free with an enormous CRACK. He turned and swung it by the rope.

It connected with the second superman on the button. The man went fifty feet into the water. Two down.

The remaining three came at him together.

Joe swung the mooring stud again. One of them reached out and caught it as casually as a man catches a ball tossed to him at short range and ripped it from Joe's hands.

All three attacked. Joe fought them. He landed good blows, hard blows, the kind that would have ended any ordinary man's evening, and the Nazi monsters absorbed them and kept coming. They were relentless in the same way he was relentless, and there were three of them, and they drove him to the ground and started kicking, and the kicks had power that ordinary kicks did not have. Each one was an event that took a frightening toll.

Joe grabbed one of the kicking boots. He gripped it with both hands, and held it and upended the man. Then he did something that would not have been possible for anyone else in this harbor. He lifted the man off the ground by his foot and swung him in a long arc and brought his head into the head of the man beside him.

The sound the two skulls made when they connected was not something that belonged in the world of ordinary men.

Two of them went down and did not move again. That left one. The leader.

He came at Joe immediately. He was fast for his size and stronger than Joe could have imagined. His hands wrapped around Joe's throat, and Joe was on the ground. The man was on top of him and squeezing with a force that was beyond human.

Joe looked up at him. The man's teeth were clenched. His eyes bulged with commitment and effort. The images began to blur at the edges as Joe's oxygen went away, the man's face becoming shapeless, and then —

A gunshot.

The man slumped sideways off Joe and onto the dock, and Joe lay there for a moment with the harbor above him and the stars above that and the sound of his own breathing finding its way back.

He looked past the fallen superman.

Sonja stood there above him, the sailor's Luger in her hand, smoke still coming from the barrel.

She was soaking wet, and she was shaking, but still the most beautiful woman Joe had ever seen. And, of course, her timing couldn't have been better.

Joe smiled and got up.

Someone else appeared.

A hand closed around Sonja's gun arm and snatched the Luger from her grip with a speed and precision that Joe recognized even as he was scrambling to his feet, because he had seen it in a ring.

Max Schmeling.

He was out of his boxing clothes and into civilian dress, and he was not hurt the way a man who had been counted out in the first round should be hurt. That told Joe something he had already been putting together for himself.

"I tried to tell the Fuhrer these lab rats would be no match for you, Joe."

Joe got to his feet. Schmeling put the Luger to Sonja's head.

"You took a dive, didn't you?" Joe asked. "You're part of this whole thing."

Schmeling smiled again. It was not the smile from the ring or from the Berchtesgaden party. It was something older than those, and more honest.

"Sometimes to lose is better than to win... While New York is out celebrating, the enemies of the Reich die."

He let that sit for a moment.

"That wasn't the real fight, Joe..."

He threw the Luger into the water and pushed Sonja away from him.

"...this is!"

Schmeling's left connected, and the right hand followed it, the thunderous right that had been studied and rehearsed and aimed at a specific angle and had found its target twice now, and Joe went into a streetlight, and the metal of it bent around the impact.

Joe staggered forward, and Schmeling caught him with an uppercut that flipped him, and he landed on his stomach, and Schmeling stood above him.

"And this time, it's to the death!"

He picked up the streetlight pole and brought it down toward Joe's head, and Joe's hands came up and caught it, and he pushed, and the force of it sent Schmeling into the side of a building, and the bricks crumbled around the point of impact.

He climbed back out. He leaped from the building and landed on Joe and threw punches, and Joe absorbed them and staggered and threw a weak jab because it was what he had available, and Schmeling countered the way Joe knew he would — the right hand, always the right hand, coming exactly as it had always come.

Joe dodged it. He stepped back, then moved inside with everything he had left, all of it going to the body, the body shots that Chappie had built into him over years of early morning sweat. Joe was more than just a powerful man. He was a fighter in the best sense of the word. He was an artist at work.

Schmeling absorbed them, and came back with combinations of his own and Joe slipped and feinted, and the fists found nothing but air.

Then Joe threw a left. Not a jab. Something larger than a jab, thrown from the shoulder with everything behind it, and it went into Schmeling's right shoulder and the sound it produced, the cracking of bones under impact, was something that would stay with everyone within earshot for the rest of their lives.

Schmeling's right arm went limp.

He looked at it. He moved it, and nothing happened. It hung there meekly. No force of will could raise it. His invincibility had lived in that arm for his entire career, and now his entire career was lying at his feet, and they both knew it.

Joe followed up. He came forward and hit him again, and again and Schmeling took it because he had no other option, one arm dead, the legs still working but working alone, and Joe administered the kind of beating that a normal man would not have survived. Schmeling was not a normal man, but he was still not enough.

A right uppercut lifted Schmeling off the ground and sent him into a parked truck, and the truck crumpled around him.

Joe took a deep, cleansing breath. His greatest nemesis vanquished, but he didn't get to enjoy it.

"Joe! President Roosevelt is holding a meeting aboard the Queen Mary! There's a torpedo heading straight for it!"

Sonja's voice. Joe turned to her, registered the information, and turned back to the harbor.

He ran for the dock edge and dove.

The water was cold and dark, and he moved through it with the efficiency of a man for whom water is simply another medium, no more hostile than air. He came around the side of the Queen Mary and saw the wake of the torpedo moving through the dark water toward the ship, relentless, massive, on a path that would not miss.

He swam straight for it.

He met it head-on and put his hands against it and pushed, and the torpedo pushed back with everything it had, which was the accumulated force of all the machinery behind it, and Joe was pushed back with it, feet churning, arms straining, the thing moving him as though his body were a minor inconvenience.

He could not stop it.

So, Joe tried to turn it. He pushed from the side, redirecting rather than resisting, and the torpedo moved a degree, then two and then three, and three degrees was not enough but it was a beginning, and Joe kept his hands on it and kept pushing, and the turn continued slowly, incrementally, the torpedo arguing with the redirection at every point. Some new technology was fighting against Joe and correcting its course.

The Queen Mary was still in the path of it. The hull was there, enormous and illuminated, and the torpedo was closing the distance quickly. Too damned quickly.

Joe thought.

He swam to the rear of the torpedo. The two propellers churned away in the water, driving the thing forward. He looked at them. He thought about what he was about to do and thought about Homer's word.

He timed it.

He reached out with both hands and grabbed the left propeller, one blade on each side, and stopped its turning. His right hand opened along the palm, and blood went into the water, but he held on because there was no alternative to holding on.

The right propeller was in control now, the asymmetry of the two propellers forcing a hard left turn. Joe held the left propeller fast and used every ounce of his strength, and the torpedo turned, and the Queen Mary's hull went past with inches between them.

He held on as the torpedo completed its turn in the Hudson River and pointed itself back toward the open ocean. He swam behind it, guiding it, one hand bleeding, the city behind him and the open water ahead, and somewhere out there, half a mile offshore, a periscope.

Joe's eyes were good in the dark. Better than good. He found it — the thin shape of the periscope in the black water, barely visible, exactly where he needed it to be.

He released the torpedo on a line straight for it.

* * *

The Queen Mary. Conference Room.

Churchill still had the floor when Donovan and Mercer came through the door at speed.

"Mr. President, we need to get you and everyone else out of here!"

Mercer grabbed Roosevelt's wheelchair and started pushing, and then there was a thunderous explosion, a concussion from somewhere off the bow that rattled through the hull and the walls and the floor.

They ran to the balcony. All of them. Mercer pushed Roosevelt to where he could see.

Out on the horizon, a fireball rose from the ocean, climbed into the night sky, and kept climbing, orange and massive.

Roosevelt looked down from the balcony at the dock below. He looked at Joe climbing out of the water. He looked at Sonja beside him. He looked at the two of them in the light of the burning horizon.

Churchill came to the railing beside him.

"What the bloody hell was that?!"

Roosevelt looked at Churchill. He smiled.

"That, Mr. Churchill, was the Brown Bomber!"

As if on cue, Joe looked up. He saw Roosevelt. He saw the others at the railing — Churchill, the Joint Chiefs, all of them looking down at a man who had just climbed out of the Hudson River with his hand bleeding and his white robe dark with water and the light of a distant explosion behind him.

Joe shot Roosevelt the A-OK sign.

Roosevelt turned to Mercer.

"Get me on my feet!"

Mercer got him up. Roosevelt stood on the balcony above the harbor and looked down at Joe Louis and saluted him. The Joint Chiefs saw him do it and followed, one by one, until every military man on the balcony had his hand raised to the visor of his hat.

Joe stood on the dock with Sonja beside him and looked up at the balcony. He looked at the salutes. He looked at the city behind him, and the burning horizon beyond it, and the Queen Mary above him, and all of it together had the quality of something that was going to be very hard to explain to most people.

A crowd was gathering. People who had been on the dock and in the streets nearby, drawn by the noise of the fight and the explosion. They were recognizing him. They were moving toward him.

He looked at Sonja. She was shivering, her hair was wet, and she had the sailor's Luger still in her hand, and she looked at him the way she had looked at him in the Beverly Hills garden in the dark, which was the way she always looked at him when she wasn't managing anything.

He was aware of the crowd. White faces, most of them. He knew what this looked like, and he knew what the country was, and he thought about Jack Johnson and Roxborough's rules and the weight of everything he had been warned about his entire life.

Then he thought about Homer.

"Hell with them!"

He pulled Sonja into his arms and kissed her. He waited for the crowd's reaction — the anger, the shouting, the thing he had always been told would come.

The crowd cheered.

It was not a polite cheer or an ambivalent one. It was the cheer of people who decided, in this moment in history, that it was time to celebrate greatness. The rules of the last 300 years no longer applied.

Joe held Sonja, and the crowd cheered, and the horizon burned, and the night went on.

* * *

Berlin. The Reich Chancellery.

Goebbels ran down the hallway on his club foot. He came to the door, braced himself, knocked, and entered.

Hitler looked up from his desk.

"My Fuhrer. I regret to inform you that our spy, Terrier, reports that the bomb has failed."

Hitler rose. His fist came down on the desk.

"How could this happen?"

Goebbels stood in the center of the room and said the only true answer to the question that he knew.

"The... the... Joe Louis."

He said nothing further. Hitler glared at him for a moment

and then began to destroy the room, the objects on the desk, the books and pictures on the shelves, the furniture, all of it receiving the attention of a man whose entire understanding of the order of things had just been contradicted by a single fact that the Nazi world view could not possibly accept.

"Are you telling me that a lone negro stopped the most powerful weapon in the history of the world?"

Goebbels did not answer. The answer was *yes*, and elaboration would only make things worse.

Chapter 13

Las Vegas. Caesars Palace, 1974.

Old Joe sat across from Bowdin in the suite, looking at the young man's face and watching the story land as a story does when it has been told well. It hit him in waves; the implications arrived after the events, each one finding its place.

Bowdin's face had been doing a number of things over the past several hours. It had been skeptical and then interested and then engaged, and then somewhere in the middle, it had crossed a line that Bowdin himself had not noticed crossing. Now, it was the face of someone who had been moved greatly and was in the process of deciding what to do about that.

He was smiling.

It was not the smile of a man who believed what he had heard. It was the smile of a man who had been thoroughly entertained by something he did not believe. It was a tall tale, like a lumberjack named Paul Bunyan creating the Great Lakes. It was a great story, but nothing more.

"Damn, Joe, you almost had me going there a couple of times!"

Joe looked at him. He said it simply, without pressure.

"You don't believe me?"

Bowdin's smile widened. He leaned back in his chair with the comfortable posture of a young man who has decided he is too clever to leave his cynicism behind. It was the 1970s, after all.

"Oh, sure, I believe you. You're the world's first black superhero; you single-handedly stopped a Nazi invasion of New York, *and* you got the girl in the end! The white girl!"

He paused.

"OK, I'll play along... Whatever happened to you and Sonja?"

Joe was quiet for a moment. He looked at the Linie Aquavit bottle on the table between them. It was nearly empty now, the clear liquid down to a finger's worth at the bottom, and the evening had been long, and the suite had grown familiar, and the tape in the recorder on the table had been turning for a very long time.

"The world just wasn't ready for us. But Sonja and me kept close and saw each other whenever we could..."

He stopped. Something moved across his face that the young man with the recorder had not seen before. It wasn't the dry humor, or the dignity, or the patience. Something older than any of those things. It was something that had been sitting under all the rest of it all evening, waiting for a moment that required it.

"...right up until a few years ago when she passed."

He picked up the small glass of Linie Aquavit and raised it. He looked at it, and then he looked through it and at whatever was on the other side of it that only he could see.

To Sonja.

He set the glass down. He looked at Bowdin. He wanted to say something more — wanted to find the combination of words that would make the young man understand that what he had just spent the evening listening to was not a story, not entertainment, not the crazy ramblings of an old fighter with too much time on his hands, who drank too much Norwegian liqueur. But he had been looking for those words his whole life, and they had not come. He was sixty years old and his knuckles hurt, and the suite was warm, and Bowdin was young, and the world was not yet ready for everything that was true about it.

He smiled.

"So, I almost had you going, huh?"

"You sure did."

"Well, just chalk it up to the crazy ramblings of an old punch-drunk pug. I enjoyed it, though."

"Me too, Joe."

Joe set his hands on his knees and pushed himself to his feet with the effort that sixty years and a thousand fights and the gravity of a life fully lived had made necessary. He was a big man, and he moved like a big man who has been carrying things for a long time and has gotten very good at making it look like nothing.

"I'll walk you out. Time to start my shift. I work as a greeter here at the casino."

"You like that job?" Bowdin asked.

Joe sensed dismissal in Bowdin's tone.

"You mean, is the work beneath me?" Joe answered. "No. I don't think it is. It's honest work, and I enjoy being with people from all walks. I like talking to them. It may not be as good as being heavyweight champ, but it beats the hell out of picking cotton or hauling ice."

Bowdin nodded and smiled.

The morning light had a special quality to it. It was Joe's favorite part of the day.

They stepped through the front doors and stopped on the

steps. Bowdin turned, and they shook hands. Bowdin felt the true power of Joe Louis arc up his arms and through his muscles. The man still has one hell of a grip, Bowdin thought.

"Thank you, Mr. Louis."

"My pleasure."

Bowdin took off down the steps and into the morning. Joe watched him go. He stood in the doorway of Caesars Palace in his greeter's uniform with his hands easy at his sides.

He was still watching when the two large men in suits stepped out from somewhere and hurried toward Bowdin with the practiced efficiency of men who had done this before and knew how quickly it needed to happen. One of them reached out and took the tape recorder and the tapes. The other one hit Bowdin, and Bowdin went down on the pavement, and they dashed off into a waiting car, got in, and the car drove away.

Bowdin lay on the pavement for a moment. He got up slowly, processing more than just the fall. He looked at the car going away. He looked at the place where the tape recorder had been.

Then he turned and looked back at the doorway.

Joe was still standing there. Still watching. Bowdin was pretty sure the man was smiling at him. Yes, he was. He could see it as the morning light landed on his face. The old son of a bitch was smiling at him.

"Sorry," Joe said. "I guess it's still too soon to talk about it."

Bowdin got up, stood on the pavement, looked at him, and understood that everything the old man had told him over the course of a long evening in a Las Vegas hotel suite was exactly what it was. It was not a story, not a performance, not the ramblings of a punch-drunk pug, but a true account of battles that were fought and won and had never been talked about since.

He shook his head slowly. The smile on his face was different from the one he had inside. It had more in it.

He stood up straight. He removed his faded baseball cap, with the Afro he had been hiding under it all evening.

Then he raised his fist.

It was a black power salute, and it was not ironic, and it was not performed. It was the gesture of a young man who had just had his understanding of the world rearranged by an old man in a hotel suite.

Joe looked at him from the doorway.

Then, slowly, he raised his own fist and returned the salute.

The two of them stood there for a moment in the morning light. The old man in the doorway and the young man on the pavement. And the moment had the quality of something that was not going to be in any history book but was going to matter, anyway.

Then Bowdin turned and walked away.

Joe watched him go.

And the morning went on.

NOTES

I remember watching a TV show as a child, and an elderly black man came on as a guest. He struggled to find his words, and, as it often is with children, I couldn't imagine that he had once been young and vital.

"Who is that old guy?" I asked my dad.

"That's Joe Louis. He's the greatest boxer who ever lived."

Who could be better than Muhammad Ali, I thought? But the name stayed with me, stored in my memory for decades without being activated.

Then, some years ago, I saw a boxing documentary in which Joe Louis was among the men discussed. This prompted a bit of research. I came away from it, awed. Not only was he the longest-tenured heavyweight boxing champion in history (a record that still stands), but his name loomed large across so many areas of American life.

He fought numerous benefit bouts that raised money for the war effort. He enlisted in the Army as a private and spoke out publicly in support of his country, which could not have been easy given that he was serving in a segregated unit, that Jim Crow was prevalent, and that racism remained intact and overt. Still, his efforts helped chip away at racial barriers and stereotyping as much as they could given the era. He also used his personal connections to support many black soldiers, one of whom turned out to be Jackie Robinson, who later broke the color barrier in Major League Baseball.

He was also a long-time devotee of golf, was an excellent player, and in 1952, became one of the first black men invited to play in a tour event, the San Diego Open. Two weeks later, he was invited to play in the Tucson Open. He shot 69 and 72, becoming the first champion from another sport to make the cut in a PGA Tour event. He was not just a strong man in the ring. He was an athlete of extraordinary skill.

Then I read about his two fights with Max Schmeling, which took place in the lead-up to World War II. The greatest fighter in the United States was fighting the greatest fighter in Germany. Schmeling had been the Heavyweight Champion of the World. Louis soon would be. It was the Allies versus the Axis powers, Roosevelt versus Hitler, and good versus evil. One could see these fights, particularly the second one, as a prelude to, or even a microcosm of, the pending war.

His importance as a historical figure was astounding. Somebody needs to make a movie, I thought. Then, I decided, why not me?

Joe Louis would be the subject of my next screenplay. The title came quickly. *The Night of the Century,* a play on Fight of the Century. It would focus on the second fight, in 1938, where Louis sought to avenge his first and only defeat at the time, which came at the hands of Max Schmeling on June 19, 1936. The structure would be fractured, moving backward and forward in time and including pertinent biographical details of Louis's life and the political ramifications of a fight that the whole world would be watching.

I read several biographies and learned that Louis had affairs with Lena Horne, Lana Turner, Sonja Henie, and many other women. He also had severe tax problems, drug problems, and health declines that happen with age.

I took it all on board as I began my outline. Still, I knew I wanted the focus of my story on that second Louis vs. Schmeling fight and the implications it had in the world at large. Joe Louis as a great American hero. He had lived an important life. When I was ready to start writing the script, I told my agent about it and how I was going to handle my story. I couldn't control my enthusiasm, so he controlled it for me.

"Spike Lee is ahead of you on this," he said. "There is no point in your doing it."

I was disappointed to say the least, but I understood the logic immediately. Spike Lee was a writer *and* a director. His package was already halfway home. He was also a much more significant figure in the film industry than I was. Add to that, Spike Lee was black, and I wasn't. To me, Joe Louis was a fascinating man and an important historical figure. To Spike Lee, Joe Louis was a vital part of his cultural history. The story belonged to him much more than it belonged to me. I dropped *The Night of the Century*.

But Joe Louis didn't go away. I thought about him all the time. Then, one night, I was having drinks with my buddy Joe Gayton. I told him the story and just started downloading all the Joe Louis facts I could think of that made him so interesting to me. Joe was also a fight fan and was also a big World War II buff. He got the power and the potential of the story right away.

Two weeks later, I made a leap that is hard to track.

What if?

I called Joe and asked the question. "What if Joe Louis was the world's first superhero?"

"And nobody has said anything about it until now because he was black," Joe answered, finishing my sentence without hesitation. That was all it took. He got it. We both immediately knew where this story was going. In the length of a phone call much of this story came into being.

It was a tall tale. Max Schmeling was the Nazi superhero made in one of Josef Mengele's lab experiments. Joe Louis's affair with Sonja Henie was perfect for our story. I knew that she and Louis had an affair. Joe knew that she had been accused of being a collaborator with the Nazis because of her close ties to Joseph Goebbels, who had released some of her movies in Germany. Then, we invented a secret plot to decapitate the leadership of the world in a dastardly Nazi attack that was planned on the night when everyone was giving all of their attention to the big fight. Joe Louis, the superhero, had to defeat Max Schmeling in the ring and then save the entire free world moments later.

We outlined and wrote the script. Ice Cube's company, Cube Vision, optioned it. It looked like it was going to get made into a feature film.

I will leave it there because the rest of the story is an anticlimax. The movie didn't get made. After a few years, the rights came back to us, and the script sat inside our computers as a file for several years.

In 2023, Joe Gayton passed away.

Then, recently, I began what I call my RunTime projects: books that read like movies. *Hyde* was the first of them. *The Brown Bomber* was the ideal follow-up. If ever there was something that looked, felt, and read like a movie, this was it.

It was strange continuing the project without Joe, but his essential contribution had already been made. My job was to translate our screenplay into a new format. I wrote the prose that turned it from a screenplay into a novel. Beyond that, I added very little new material. The story exists almost exactly as Joe and I conceived it.

As I went through the scenes, I remembered so many of the laughs we had while working on the outline and writing those early drafts, how we tried to top each other and make the other laugh. Simple things like when I wrote "Joe tosses Sonja Henie over the wall at the White House," and Joe added, "She spun once in mid air and landed, well, like a world-class figure skater would land on ice."

The other thing that really struck me was the emotional impact and how alive Joe was in my head through this process. I wrote as if I were seeking his approval, trying to channel him as best I could for the right words or phrases.

Then, there was this. Joe Gayton, Joe Louis, Josef Goebbels, and Joseph Mengele were all significant characters in the story. I was writing and reading the name "Joe" a lot. And I was glad for it.

Regarding the story itself, it is a tall tale. It was never intended as a biography. Though we wanted to be accurate in principle, particularly in establishing Joe Louis as a great American hero, we took liberties with the facts, and we know we did. We changed the order of the first Louis/Schmeling fight and the Louis/Braddock fight because it worked better dramatically. In real life, Schmeling never became champion a second time as it is played in this book. Again, because we saw this as a tall tale, we took license to make our story as dramatic as possible.

So, there is a good bit of revisionist history here. There are also more than a few elements made up from whole cloth.

Though Joe did considerable work for the US government during the war, he did not work for Wild Bill Donovan and the OSS, unless, of course, that still remains classified. Hoover did not spy for the Nazis. Joe Gayton and I just didn't like him, so we painted him as a villain. Joe Louis *did* have an affair with Sonja Henie. How long it lasted and how serious it was are matters of debate. Sonja Henie *was* accused of having Nazi sympathies. That is also true.

Then, of course, there is Max Schmeling. He was not a Nazi superhuman built in a lab as depicted in our book. I want to make that clear immediately to shut down any crazed conspiracy theorists who might be reading. He was an honorable man who resisted joining the Nazi Party despite great pressure to do so. Though he was drafted and served as a paratrooper, he never supported the Nazi regime and was viewed with suspicion by them.

After the war, he and Joe Louis developed a deep and lasting friendship. Schmeling became a wealthy executive with the Coca-Cola Company, helped Louis through his tax problems, and served as a pallbearer at his funeral. He remained married to actress Annie Ondra until her passing in 1987.

Max Schmeling died on February 2, 2005, at age 99.

As for Joe Louis. He was already a great American hero. He didn't need us to expand his legend in any way. Still, if this book, in even a limited way, can revive an interest in learning the truth about him among future generations, it can only be a good thing. His was an extraordinary life. And if Spike Lee ever makes his biography of Joe Louis, I will be first in line to see it.

Joe Louis died on April 12, 1981. He was buried in Arlington

National Cemetery in Arlington, Virginia. He was interred with full military honors. His tomb is a short walk from the tomb of the Unknown Soldier.

About the Author

Joe Gayton was a film director, screenwriter, and producer in Hollywood for over 40 years. His credits are varied and extensive. He wrote, or co-wrote, the following movies: *Faster, Uncommon Valor, Bulletproof, Shout* and others. He wrote and directed *Sweet Jane, Mind Ripper,* and *Warm Summer Rain.* He also co-created the hit Western TV series, *Hell on Wheels,* with his brother, Tony Gayton.

Patrick Cirillo is a screenwriter and novelist. His feature screen credits include *Tears of the Sun* and *Homer & Eddie* (among others). His novels include *LORA: Artificial Intelligence Just Got Real... and She's Lovely, Wyatt and the Duke, The Lie That Kills,* and the *Extraordinary Souls* duology. He also co-wrote the nonfiction book *True Stories from the Dark Side of Sports* with his brother Ernie Cirillo.

You can connect with me on:

https://www.facebook.com/profile.php?id=100091810331570

Also by Patrick Cirillo & Joe Gayton

LORA: Artificial Intelligence Just Got Real... And She's Lovely

Kenton Bean just wanted someone to share his life. He got so much more — a student, a companion, a confidant, and a love that would challenge everything he believed about what it means to be human. He also never expected that they would become the focal point in the coming revolution between AI and mankind.

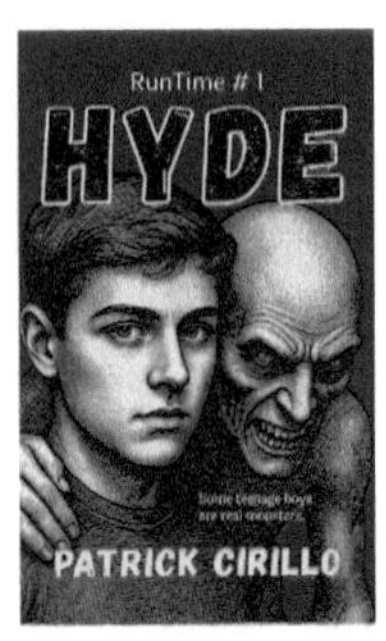

HYDE

Book 1, RunTime Series. AJ Pierce is a handsome, popular junior at an elite Los Angeles high school. Good grades. Good friends. Good life. Then the past catches up with him in the form of a father he barely knew.

Henry Jekyll was a brilliant geneticist who accidentally created the virus that destroyed him. Now, through a genetic mutation, AJ has been infected with his father's creation. And what destroyed Henry Jekyll is starting to happen to his son.

EXTRAORDINARY SOULS, WYRDWORKING

In a world of the ordinary, a new breed of mankind has emerged — twisted, brilliant, dangerous, steeped in the magic of the ancients, and terrifyingly free. They are the Extraordinary Souls. And they do not want to merely fit in. They seek vengeance against a mankind that once stoned, drowned, and burned them at the stake... a mankind that feared them and sought to exterminate them.

THE LIE THAT KILLS

Young Casey Smith lied to federal agents to protect the ex-con father she loves. Now powerful people want her dead.

Her lie was supposed to be harmless. Instead, it injects Casey straight into the bloodstream of a criminal conspiracy involving a Mexican cartel, corrupt federal officials and two terrifying sicarios assigned to kill her.

WYATT & THE DUKE

WYATT & THE DUKE brings to vivid life one of Hollywood's most enduring legends, that an aging Wyatt Earp was the real-life mentor to a promising young Western star named Marion Morrison.

Hollywood, 1927. The frontier is officially closed. But the West isn't finished yet—it's just moved onto a soundstage.

TRUE STORIES FROM THE DARK SIDE OF SPORTS

In *True Stories from the Dark Side of Sports: Volume One*, authors Patrick Cirillo and Ernie Cirillo pull back the curtain on the secret world behind the stadium lights; a world filled with crime, corruption, tragedy, and the fragile human beings caught inside it.

www.ingramcontent.com/pod-product-compliance
Lightning Source LLC
LaVergne TN
LVHW090519110826
845146LV00003B/922